Seeing Melissa's joy at his words made it difficult to speak the words Dan knew he must say.

"And now, Melissa, it's time for us to say good-bye. I'll never be able to thank you for all you've done for me or to tell you what you've come to mean to me." He reached for her hands, unmindful of the amused stares of people passing by. "I'll never forget you, darling girl. Never."

Melissa's knees wouldn't support her any longer. She slumped down on the hard earth and fought a losing battle with her tears. She buried her face in her hands and sobbed.

Dan knelt down beside her. "Don't cry, Melissa. Someday I'll get my life back together, and when I do, I'll come back to find you."

"No, you won't," she sobbed. "I know I'll never see you again. Oh, Dan, take me with you, please."

"You know I can't do that, Melissa. Not until I have a place for you. But you can do one thing for me."

Melissa lifted her tear-stained face and looked at him through watery eyes. "Anything. I'll do anything to help you."

"Promise you'll pray for me. And keep reading God's Word. Just remember that He has a plan for your life, and if you trust Him, He will show you the way." He took her hands and pulled her to her feet. "Wipe your tears, Melissa, and go into the commissary to get your supplies. I don't want you to watch me le

MUNCY G. CHAPMAN has four children who magically became eight (i.e., their spouses) and then was blessed with eleven grandchildren. All live in Florida. She says she is married to the most wonderful man in the world with whom she recently celebrated their golden wedding anniversary. Muncy likes to sew, cook, play the piano, and, of course, write. She works with the children in her church and also with the shut-ins as a "Caring Caller." She enjoys writing with her husband. He likes the research, and she likes choosing the words.

Books by Muncy G. Chapman

HEARTSONG PRESENTS
HP266—What Love Remembers
HP319—Margaret's Quest
HP361—The Name Game
HP422—Condo Mania
HP556—Red Hills Stranger

The Way Home

Muncy G. Chapman

Heartsong Presents

Lovingly dedicated to Gammy's little girls:
Kelly, Janelle, Kristen, Kori, and Maria

A note from the Author:
I love to hear from my readers! You may correspond with me by writing:

Muncy G. Chapman
Author Relations
PO Box 719
Uhrichsville, OH 44683

ISBN 1-59310-624-6

THE WAY HOME

Our mission is to publish and distribute inspirational products offering exceptional value and biblical encouragement to the masses.

All of the characters and events in this book are fictitious. Any resemblance to actual persons, living or dead, or to actual events is purely coincidental.

All scripture quotations are taken from the King James Version of the Bible.

PRINTED IN THE U.S.A.

one

Florida Territory—1840

Melissa Malcolm tripped over a fallen pine tree and fell headlong onto the soggy soil of the Florida Territory. Because her fall was cushioned by a deep layer of pine needles and oak leaves, the only things that suffered were her pride and her pinafore. How could she ever expect to find a rabbit for supper unless she kept her mind on her task and her eyes focused on the ground in front of her?

The truth was, as badly as she and her mother needed a bit of meat for their stew pot, Melissa hated hurting the innocent little woods creatures. She reminded herself over and over again that rabbits had all but ruined their winter garden, yet when she saw their cute little furry faces and stubby tails, her heart melted. She felt the same way about squirrels, too. Melissa might as well face it—as a hunter, she was a miserable failure.

Climbing out of her soft, feathery bed this morning, she had promised herself that today would be different. One look at her frail mother bent over their wood-burning stove, stirring a pot of grits for breakfast, convinced Melissa that she had to find some way to provide meat for their table. She had packed a few biscuits into the roomy pockets of her homespun pinafore, kissed her mother on the cheek, and set out to find something for supper.

Melissa picked herself up from the ground and retrieved her slingshot from a few feet away. The stones she had collected along the way were now scattered and hidden within the dense blanket of leaves. Heaving a sigh, she scavenged the ground for more to replace them.

On moccasin-covered feet, she crept through the dense forest in search of food. This time she would be more careful. She did keep a closer watch on her steps, but her mind continued to wander.

How much longer would her father be gone? She wished the logging camps were stationary so that he could remain in one place long enough for his family to join him. Papa had been away for weeks. He didn't even know how Melissa had nursed her mother through the frightening, critical days of influenza last month. Although her mother had miraculously survived, Melissa knew they had a long way to go before Mama would be strong and healthy again.

Hearing a sound of rushing water, Melissa realized she was nearing the Fenholloway River. My, she had wandered a long way from home! How pleasant it would be to sit on the riverbank and rest for a few moments. She couldn't allow herself the luxury of a long stop because she still had a job to do. Picturing her stick-thin mother shuffling about the house this morning strengthened Melissa's resolve not to return home empty-handed.

Choosing a large rock overlooking the peaceful river, she spread her skirts and sat down. With elbows on her knees, she propped her chin in her hands and studied her reflection in the drifting current. Why couldn't she have inherited her mother's pretty blond curls instead of straight brown hair that hung down past her shoulders like a horse's mane? She pushed it back from her face and continued to analyze her features. If she could have chosen, she would have picked dark brown eyes like her father's. Papa's eyes always reminded Melissa of rich, dark chocolate. But instead, she was stuck with eyes as green and common as ordinary grass. The few freckles on her nose didn't help her appearance very much, either. She certainly didn't resemble the fashionable ladies she studied in her well-worn copy of *Ladies Companion*.

A sudden splash and a glint of silver disturbed her reflection, giving Melissa a new idea. If she could catch a fish for dinner, that would be almost as good as a rabbit. She pulled a stale biscuit from her pocket, broke off a piece for bait, and ate the remainder.

She slipped out of her moccasins and felt the cool earth beneath her feet, squishy between her toes. Sliding down the bank, she searched the water for a shallow spot. Hoisting her skirts, she stepped onto a sandbar. A scant four inches deep, the water felt cold on her legs, causing her to shiver. Using slender, agile fingers, she made a tight ball of dough and dropped it into the stream beside her feet. Then she loaded her slingshot and waited. "Come on, little fishy. Try my nice, homemade biscuits." She stood as still as a fence post, hoping to lure the fish into the shallows.

As though to taunt her, the elusive fish flashed his silvery fins and swam in a wide circle around her feet, but not once did he venture from his secure depths.

"Bother!" she muttered. This was a waste of time, and time was becoming a precious commodity. She climbed the riverbank and slipped wet feet into her leather moccasins. She trudged on through the woods, still hoping to find something to nourish her mother back to health. Her own rumbling stomach added to her incentive.

In the distance, she heard a shot. That hunter would likely have a lot more success than Melissa with her homemade slingshot. When Papa was home, he often took his rifle into the woods to provide them with ample supplies of meat, not only for their immediate needs but also for making dried jerky. The deer jerky he made during his last trip home was supposed to carry them through the winter, but most of it had long since been consumed. How much longer would she and her mother have to wait for Papa's return?

She continued her search but soon decided all the rabbits and squirrels must be sleeping. Although she had walked until the sun was halfway across the sky, she had not spotted a single creature. She might as well turn back and go home. Maybe she would see something along the way. If not, she would try again after the sun went down.

Hearing a noise, Melissa crouched behind a stand of palmettos and peered through the fronds. Again she heard the noise, but it didn't sound like a rabbit or a squirrel. Suppose it was a bear or a panther? She knew her slingshot would be poor defense against a wild animal. Her heart raced, and she slumped lower in the bushes. There! She heard it again. It sounded like a low moan. Not an animal moan, either, but a *human* one.

Melissa knew that the Florida Territory was rampant with outlaws and renegade Indians. From the stories she had heard, she would rather meet a wild animal than either of those.

Should she make a run for it and hope to get away? There was no way that would work. The sounds came from very close at hand, and she was a good two hours away from her homestead. She couldn't hope to outrun an Indian or an outlaw, much less a bear or a panther. Better to try to stay hidden and hope for the danger to pass.

Minutes seemed like hours, yet the intermittent cries continued. Melissa's legs ached from her cramped position, but still she made no movement that would reveal her whereabouts. It seemed to Melissa that the source of the moans was growing weaker, until at last all sounds ceased.

This could be a trick, she thought. Still, she had few options. She couldn't remain here until dark. She eased herself up and looked around in every direction but saw nothing that gave her a clue. She selected her largest stone and held it in the center of her slingshot, ready for whatever she might find. Her heart beat wildly. Stealthily, she crept from her hideaway and moved toward the place where the noise had emanated.

Circling a huge pine tree, she stopped and gasped at the sight before her. Not a bear. Not a panther. Not even a rabbit or squirrel. Sprawled on the ground was a full-grown man, and from all appearances, he was dead.

Still suspecting a trick, she edged closer, keeping her slingshot drawn and aimed at the man's head. She touched his body gingerly with the toe of her moccasin, but his inert body gave no sign of life.

Tucking her ineffective weapon into her pocket, Melissa knelt on the ground beside him and tried to turn him over.

He was a large man, and she had difficulty moving him; but at last she was able to roll him over and get a good look at his face. Blond hair fell across his forehead, almost concealing an ominous purple lump. His shirt of blue homespun linen was covered with fresh blood. Maybe this was the hunter whose shot she had heard earlier, and perhaps he had been attacked by his prey.

She thought him dead until she saw a flutter of his eyelids and caught a glimpse of his eyes—the bluest she had ever seen. "What happened to you? Are you all right?" *Foolish question!*

He responded with a weak moan—the same sound that had frightened her earlier. What could she do to help him? She was miles from the nearest homestead. No one could possibly hear her cries. Still, just in case, she yelled with all her might. "Help! Someone please help us!" But although she shouted again and again, the only sound that came back to her was the soft rustle of the wind whistling gently through the pine trees.

She unbuttoned his shirt with trembling fingers. She must locate his wound and attempt to stanch the flow of blood.

He had already lost a goodly amount of it. No wonder he was as weak as a newborn colt. The knot on his forehead suggested he had hit his head when he fell, but this seemed to be the least of his maladies.

She gasped at the sight of the wound just below his shoulder. If she was any judge of injuries, she would guess that this was a gunshot wound that went clear through his body. Had he accidentally shot himself while hunting? But if so, where was his gun?

Using her teeth to rip off a piece of her muslin skirt, she tore a wide strip of cloth from its hemline. She stuffed the fabric into the wound and applied pressure, just as she had seen her mother do on that day when her father had cut his foot while chopping wood for their stove.

I can't go off and leave him here, she thought. *If he's not dead now, he soon will be.* She slid her hands beneath his shoulders and tried to lift him, but she might as well have tried to move that tall cypress tree towering over them. This man was at least six feet tall and had a robust build. There was no way she could carry him. Unless. . .

A plan began to take shape in her mind. Years ago she had learned a skill from her Seminole friend, Little Fawn. Oh, how she missed her dear little red-skinned companion. The two girls had played together for endless, glorious hours in the woods as children until, in 1836, Andrew Jackson had forced all the Seminoles out of the Florida Territory and transported them to Oklahoma. Four years had passed since they last saw each other. Melissa often wondered if Little Fawn had found happiness in her new home.

Surveying her surroundings, Melissa saw a patchwork of trees felled by lightning. She needed two young saplings light enough to pull yet strong enough to hold a heavy body.

After selecting two slender, green poles, Melissa positioned them next to the unconscious victim. She found a few smaller limbs to serve as crosspieces. Then she gathered palmetto fronds, pulling them off the bushes until her hands began to bleed. She would have to make a pallet for this man if she intended to move him.

She pulled a wad of cord from her pocket, cord she had brought in anticipation of the wild game she would capture and string up for her stew pot. Working as quickly as her nimble fingers would allow, she lashed the palm fronds to the makeshift stretcher, knowing all the while that time was of the essence and that the toughest job was still ahead of her.

Taking a deep breath, she used all her strength to push the man onto his side so that she could slide the crude pallet beneath him. His spasmodic groans encouraged her. At least he was still alive!

When his body was positioned on the palm fronds, Melissa stood between the front ends of the sapling poles and tried to pick them up. This was going to be even harder than she had expected. How could she hope to pull this man through the dense woods all the way to her cottage? Still, she knew she had to try. The alternative would be to leave him here at the mercy of wild animals who would think of him as a tasty feast. She shuddered to think of it.

With her body between the two poles and her hands gripping the rough bark, she began to pull, just as she had seen their old mule pull her father's plow over the unyielding Florida ground. Living her entire twenty years in a rugged, outdoor environment had acclimated Melissa to hard work, and she possessed a strength that her small stature belied. She strained and grunted, and at last she was rewarded by a slight forward movement as the pallet began to slide over slick pine needles and wet oak leaves.

Progress was slow. Navigating around the trunks of dense trees proved difficult, and Melissa was forced to pause periodically to catch her breath. Every time she stopped, one look at the stranger's ashen face forced her to persevere. There was little chance she could keep him alive until she reached her home, but at least she and her mother could give the poor man a decent burial.

Where had he come from? She knew most of the settlers in the north Florida woods, and she was quite sure she had never seen this man before. Had she seen him, it was unlikely that she would ever have forgotten him. She remembered again his eyes—eyes the color of a shimmering, cloudless sky.

Expensive leather boots protected his feet, and his clothes, although dirty from his fall, bore the mark of a gentleman. There were some larger ranches to the south, but surely he couldn't have walked that far. She had searched the ground for signs of a horse, but the thick carpet of wet leaves on the ground would have obscured any tracks. It was barely possible his horse could have wandered off without him.

Melissa's arms and legs ached, and her head swirled. Perspiration trickled down her forehead, and her breath came in torturous puffs and pants; but still she plowed on toward home. What would her mother think? She probably had a pot of water boiling on the stove already, expecting her daughter to bring home meat for their supper. How would Mama react when she saw what Melissa had brought home instead?

two

Just when Melissa was sure she could not move forward another step, she caught a glimpse of silver smoke curling above the treetops and knew that she was almost home. With her last remaining shred of energy, she managed to drag her heavy burden through the front gate. There she dropped her makeshift litter and abandoned it. With great effort, she stumbled toward the house and collapsed in a heap on the front steps.

She was completely spent. She wanted to call out to her mother for help, but she didn't have enough breath left to force the words from her mouth. Instead, she pillowed her head on her arms and inhaled deep gulps of air.

She heard the creak of a screen door, followed by scuffling steps. She knew her mother was nearby, but for the life of her, she couldn't speak a word.

"What is it, child?" When Melissa felt her mother's arms enfold her, all the tension that had been building up all morning was suddenly released, erupting in great, wracking sobs. "Tell me, Melissa. What's wrong? Are you hurt?"

Melissa claimed her second wind. "No, Mama. I'm all right. Just plumb worn out, that's all. Look yonder by the gate, and you'll see what's wrong."

The concerned woman followed her daughter's command and peered across the yard, using her hand to shield her eyes from the late afternoon sun. "What—I mean, *who* is that?"

Melissa's words came out slowly as her strength began to return. "I don't know, Mama. I found him in the woods where Daniel Creek branches out from the Fenholloway River."

"Why in the world did you bring him *here*, Melissa?" As she spoke, the surprised woman moved cautiously toward the gate for a closer look, and Melissa rose and followed her.

"He was hurt, Mama." Melissa bent over the inert form and watched for a sign of life. "I think he's been shot. I doubt he's even still alive." When her mother continued to gape at the man and say nothing, Melissa pleaded for understanding. "I couldn't just leave him in the woods to die alone, could I?"

Having recovered from her initial shock, the frail woman moved close to Melissa and put her arms around her shoulders "Of course you couldn't, honey. It's too bad you didn't ride Dolly this morning."

"That old mare? She's slower than molasses in January, and besides, I was afraid she'd scare away any rabbits I might find. Anyway, I don't think I could have gotten that man up on a horse. It's just as well I was walking. It was hard enough getting him around all the tree trunks."

"I suppose you're right." She circled the still body and leaned over to get a closer look. "We'll have to get help to bury him, though. He appears to be a very large man. Where did you get that pallet, and how did you ever manage to get it here all the way from the river?"

Melissa ignored her mother's questions for the moment. She stooped over the man and placed her fingers on his neck, eagerly searching for a pulse. *Please let him be alive!* She was rewarded by a faint response at her fingertips. "Mama, he's not dead! He's still alive. Help me get him into the house."

"The house? You mean *our* house? Melissa, you know we can't take this strange man into our house. Why, for all we know, he may be a dangerous outlaw!"

Melissa moved to the front of the litter and began to pick up the poles again. "Look at him, Mama. Does he look like he could harm us? If you can't help me, just hold the door open, and I'll do it myself."

Although her head, her arms and legs, and her back rebelled, Melissa possessed a strong determination that overrode her physical limitations. Even if her mother had wanted to help, her depleted strength could give little but moral support. No, Melissa would have to move the man herself.

Getting him up the steps was the hardest part. Relenting for the moment, Mama brought out her ironing board to form a crude ramp. Melissa pulled while her mother pushed, and at last the two women managed to get him across the threshold and into their parlor. "That's far enough for now," Melissa said. "We can move him to the bed later." She expected her mother to remind her that the only two beds in the house belonged to Melissa and her parents, but Mama said nothing.

"Is there any water on the stove? We need to clean up his wound and dress it properly. I don't know how long he's been like this."

Mama turned to the kitchen and returned with a pan of warm water and a stack of clean rags. "And here's a cup of sugar we can use to draw out infection," she said.

Melissa was on her knees, struggling to peel the shirt from the stranger's body. "I'm sorry I didn't get anything for supper, Mama. I tried to get a fish, but he was too slippery to catch. I never did see a rabbit or a squirrel."

All the while she talked, her hands never stopped. She dipped a square of clean cloth into the warm water and began very gently to wash the stranger's face. She thought she saw an eyelid flutter. Did she just imagine that quick flash of blue the shade of a cloudless summer sky?

Mama began working his boots from his feet. One ankle was badly swollen, making the task extremely difficult. "Oh, honey, I've been so taken up with this man, I plumb forgot to tell you the good news."

Melissa raised her head and glanced at her mother. "Is

Papa coming home?" she asked hopefully.

"No, it's not that. But it's almost that good. Don't you smell that delicious aroma coming from the kitchen? That nice Harrison Blake came by and brought us a big venison roast. I declare, I think he came by just to see you. He seemed mighty disappointed when I told him you weren't here."

Melissa wrinkled up her nose. *Harrison Blake!* She knew he had asked Papa for permission to pay court, and Papa had been all too quick to agree. Didn't her feelings count for anything?

Harrison Blake lived on a neighboring ranch, one of the largest spreads in the territory. He reminded Melissa of a giant hawk, with his long, beaklike nose and his steely gray eyes. He was twice her age, and being in his presence gave her a creepy feeling. She avoided him whenever possible.

How lucky for her that she had been away when he came to call. If Mama liked him so much, let *her* entertain him. But Melissa's extreme distaste for the man wouldn't keep her from enjoying fresh meat in their stew tonight. Tantalizing smells began to drift in from the kitchen, and Melissa's stomach growled in anticipation.

Melissa took their visitor's bloodstained shirt into the kitchen and put it in a pan of cold water to soak. Then she returned to the parlor and knelt down to continue bathing the bruised arms of the wounded man. "We need to put something on his shoulders. He'll have a chill down here on the floor this way."

Mama gave a skeptical appraisal. "We don't have a thing in the house that will fit those broad shoulders," she said. "Your father's clothes would be much too small."

Melissa mentally measured his massive frame. "How about one of Papa's nightshirts?" she suggested. "They're real big, aren't they?"

Mama looked doubtful but went into the bedroom to look for one.

Melissa had almost finished his ablutions when she looked at his face and saw that he was awake, watching her with wide-eyed wonder. "Who are you?" he asked bluntly.

Melissa's heart skipped a beat. She had feared that he would never regain consciousness. His eyes were just as blue as she remembered them. Eyes like that could turn a girl's heart to mush. When he spoke, she noted a slight separation between his two front teeth. "Melissa Malcolm," she replied. "I was hunting in the woods when I found you. Where did you come from? What happened to you?"

The man stared at her in amazement. A frown wrinkled his brow. "I—I don't know."

"Don't try to talk," Melissa said, observing his distress. "You've been badly injured. Just try to rest now, and we'll wait until you're stronger to find out all the answers." Melissa poured a generous layer of sugar over the open wound, noting that the man clenched his teeth and grimaced. She slid a strip of clean cotton beneath his neck, bringing it over his right shoulder and across his chest, securing the ends in a knot below his left arm. From the size and location of the wound, she guessed that the bullet had passed all the way through his shoulder. She tried to be as gentle as she could, but with every movement, a soft moan escaped his lips.

Mama scurried into the room carrying a voluminous flannel nightshirt. "Is he awake?" she asked. "I thought I heard voices."

"Yes, but he's very weak. Let's not bother him with questions until he's stronger." Together the two women slipped the clean gown beneath his body and worked his arms into the sleeves, leaving the unbuttoned cuffs to hang just below his elbows. The buttons and buttonholes did not meet across his chest, either, but that was just as well, because it left his wound accessible for continued care.

Seeing him shiver, Melissa pulled a crocheted afghan from the back of a chair and covered him to keep him warm. For now, she had done all that she could. She stood back and watched him close his eyes and drift back to peaceful sleep.

"When he wakes up again, let's try to give him some of the broth from our stew pot," she suggested. "That should be nourishing. There's no telling when he ate last."

"What a blessing that Harrison brought that venison," Mama declared. "He's such a thoughtful man." She glanced at her daughter out of the corner of her eye as if to measure her reaction. "My, just smell that stew simmering on the stove. I added some carrots and onions from the garden, and I crushed up some basil and parsley to give it extra flavor. It's set my mouth a-watering. I can make a pan of corn bread to go with it."

"That sounds wonderful, Mama. I'd like that. But I don't think we should try to give the stranger anything but broth tonight. His body has suffered quite a shock, and we don't want to do anything that would worsen his condition." Melissa carried the pan of red-tinged bathwater out the front door and emptied it onto her roses.

It's all so very odd, she thought. *A strange man seemed to drop out of nowhere, right into my lap.* It was almost like a sign—Little Fawn would have called it an omen. Melissa wished Little Fawn were here. Maybe she could tell her the meaning of it all.

Melissa put away the extra rags and towels and cleaned the floor around her patient's pallet. "We'll have to move him into bed next time he wakes up," she said.

Mama put her hands on her hips and looked at her daughter in exasperation. "Melissa, you know we don't have a bed for him. I'm afraid he'll just have to stay on this pallet on the floor until he's strong enough to leave."

As though she hadn't heard, Melissa went to her small room, pulled down her quilts, and stripped the sheets from her feather mattress. "Mama, I need to use our extra sheets. I'll wash mine and hang them on the line tomorrow, but there's no way I can get them dry tonight."

Mama scowled. She made it plain that she was less than happy about the arrangement, but she did as her daughter asked and pulled down their only set of spare sheets from the closet shelf. "I don't know what your father would say about all this," she mumbled. "I just hope we get this man up on his feet and out of here before Cleve comes home."

Melissa put clean muslin sheets on her feather tick and covered them with a patchwork quilt. She emptied her pitcher and refilled it with fresh water before setting it on the dresser beside her porcelain washbowl. She slid her chamber pot out of sight beneath the bed and turned back one corner of the covers. This room had been hers alone for all of her twenty years, but now she was relinquishing it to a mysterious stranger.

She returned to the parlor and saw that he was resting peacefully on his pallet, so she decided not to disturb him again until later.

Melissa didn't have time to think about being tired herself. She went to the barn to take care of the livestock. The sun had set, and dusk began to fall. Although spring was just around the corner, the March night air still had a bite to it. She didn't want Mama to get a chill, and she wanted to keep her new patient warm, too. She brought in a bundle of oak logs from the woodpile so that she could get a fire started early in the morning.

She took their three water jugs outside, filled each of them with fresh, clean water from the pump, and carried them back into the kitchen. Mama was beginning to show the signs of overexertion, and Melissa wanted to send her off to bed right after supper. This had been an unusual day—a strain on the both of them. She was sure a good night's sleep would take care of her own fatigue, but she must be on guard against a relapse of her mother's recent struggle with influenza.

Melissa lit one of their big lard-oil lamps and set it on the table. The venison stew continued to steep on the wood-burning stove while Melissa set the table for supper. Mama took down her cast-iron spider from a hook on the wall and filled it with batter for corn bread. By the time the two women sat down for their evening meal, their little cottage was warm and cozy.

As soon as the meal was over, Melissa ladled out a bowl of rich broth. "Just leave all the cleanup for me, Mama. I'll need your help in getting our visitor fed and put to bed. After that, I hope you'll turn in, too. You do look a bit tired."

Mama stiffened. "Our visitor? I hardly think we should call him that, Melissa. It's not like we invited him to come here."

"What then?" Melissa queried with a mischievous grin. "We can't call him 'family.' I know! Let's give him a name."

Mama was in no mood for Melissa's jokes. "I'm sure he already has a name. I can't imagine he would want a new one."

"Of course he has one," Melissa agreed, "but we don't know what it is, now do we? Let's see. Since I found him close to Daniel Creek, I think I'll call him Dan." She studied her mother for reaction, but seeing none, she continued, "Come on, Mama. Help me get Dan to sip a little of this broth."

"I suppose we must," Mama agreed. Rising from the table, she followed Melissa into the living room, carrying the lamp along with her.

Melissa was pleased to see that the man she now called Dan had awakened and seemed to focus his eyes on her. She knelt beside him. "Are you feeling better?" She placed her hand on his forehead. "No fever. That's a good sign. We've brought you some warm broth for your supper. Try to eat some of this, and maybe it will help you regain some of your strength."

He continued to watch her in silence. Melissa was glad she had heard him utter a few words. At least she knew he *could* speak and would talk to them when he was ready. "Mama, can you put your hand behind his head and lift him up just a little? I don't want him to choke on this broth."

Mama dropped to her knees and slid her hand beneath his head. She tilted his head a few inches from the floor, and he strained to help.

When Melissa spooned a bit of broth between his lips, he swallowed and rewarded her with a weak smile, revealing two deep dimples in his cheeks. "Mm."

Encouraged, she continued to feed him small sips, pausing between each spoonful. Little by little, the level of the broth receded in the bowl until only a few drops remained. Mama lowered his head, and he lay back obviously exhausted from the effort. He silently mouthed a thank-you, but the look of appreciation radiating from his incredibly blue eyes was more than enough thanks to satisfy Melissa.

"We'll let you rest for a while before we try to move you," she said. "In a bit, we want to get you into bed, where you can get a good night's sleep. Maybe by morning you'll be refreshed enough to answer some of our questions." Had he even heard her? His steady, even breathing indicated that Dan had already fallen back to sleep.

❧

Much later, after she had tended to all her chores, Melissa lay curled up on the settee in the parlor, cuddled in one of her mother's handmade quilts. Although she was tired to the bone, sleep eluded her. So much had happened this day, and she had a peculiar intuition that her life would never be the same again.

Getting Dan into the bed had not been as difficult as she had expected and certainly not as hard as getting him up the front steps had been. He had rallied enough to help propel himself onto the bed, even with an ankle swollen to almost double a normal size.

Who was this strange man she called Dan? Every time she looked into his astounding eyes or placed her hand on his forehead, it seemed as though some magnetic thread connected them, yet in reality, she didn't even know his name.

three

When the sun came up, Melissa woke with a start. For just a moment, she couldn't imagine why her bed felt so cramped and unyielding or why every muscle and bone in her body ached. Then she realized she had traded her soft feather mattress for the small horsehair settee in the parlor and that her body was protesting the unusually strenuous activities of the day before. She stood and stretched to get a few of the kinks out of her spine, shivering in the cool morning air.

Her first thoughts were of Dan. Had he managed to survive the night, or would she have to dig a grave for him today? She grabbed the afghan off the back of the chair to wrap around her shoulders and padded across the wood plank floor on cold, bare feet.

She peeked through a crack in the door, and her heart skipped a beat. He lay just as she had left him the night before. He hadn't moved an inch. Was he still alive? She was almost afraid to look closer.

But as she moved nearer to the bed, she saw the steady rise and fall of his chest and knew with a certainty that her Dan was still alive. She placed the palm of her hand against his forehead and was relieved to feel that his body temperature still seemed to be normal. The angry-looking bump on his forehead, though discolored, appeared to be receding.

His face in peaceful repose prompted her to brush aside a stray lock of his blond hair, letting her fingers linger on his cheek. The touch of his flesh ignited a strange quickening of her pulse.

When she withdrew her hand, she was elated to see

his eyelids flicker. Then he opened them wide and stared at Melissa with those incredible blue eyes. Looking into them, Melissa felt her heart pounding so hard she thought he must surely be able to hear it. "Good morning," she finally managed to stammer, but as quickly as he had opened his eyes, he closed them. The only answer to her greeting was the rhythm of his steady breathing.

She crept back toward the kitchen, slipping her feet into moccasins along the way, and started a fire in the cold iron stove.

In minutes, the kindling caught and spread; the flames crackled and lapped against the pieces of oak as Melissa fed them. Soon, welcome warmth began to radiate throughout the small kitchen. Melissa filled the coffeepot with water and added a handful of coffee grounds before she set it on the stove to boil. In another pan, she boiled water for oatmeal, hoping to have a hot breakfast ready before her mother woke up.

Maybe Mama would be hungry today. Her appetite had waned pitifully during her debilitating illness, and she was as thin as a fence post. Melissa tried to think of ways to tempt her with nourishing meals, hoping to add flesh to her bones and color to her cheeks before Papa's return.

And what about Dan? Would he be ready for solid food today? As soon as she dressed, she would go outside to see if the hens had laid any eggs for their morning meal. Flossie the cow had been stingy with her milk of late, but with a little luck, Melissa would coax her into filling her pail this morning.

As the sun continued to rise, the little house began to fill with light. Melissa could hear her mother in the bedroom, getting ready for the day. The fire in the stove had begun to remove the chill from the rest of the house, and the smell of fresh coffee permeated the air.

Melissa dressed quickly and tiptoed in to check on Dan

once again. Although he opened his eyes from time to time, his face showed no signs of emotion. Had he actually spoken to her last night? Now he seemed to have lapsed into a coma. Melissa had read about people who stayed in a coma for years. Was this to be Dan's dismal fate, as well?

Last night she had looked through his pockets for some shred of evidence that would shed light on his identity but found not a single clue. Somewhere a family probably watched and waited for him to come home. How could she locate them to let them know he was safe?

After tending to the livestock, Melissa sat at the kitchen table across from her mother. "Shall I fry you an egg?" she asked. "I gathered six nice ones this morning."

"No, honey. This oatmeal and cup of coffee are all I need. How did the strange—um, Dan fare the night? Have you looked in on him today?"

Melissa stirred a spoonful of molasses into her bowl of oatmeal and added a generous splash of cream, still warm from the morning milking. "He hasn't changed at all. How long do you think he'll stay like this? I sure wish he'd wake up and talk to us."

Mama nodded thoughtfully. "We've got to find out where he came from and notify his family. We can't keep him here with us."

"I know that, Mama, but what else can we do?"

"Melissa, I can see you've already grown fond of this man, but you have to remember, he's not like a pet dog or cat that we can take in and keep forever. He's a real person, and he belongs somewhere else."

Yes, Melissa admitted to herself. *Mama's right. Even in this short time, I have grown quite fond of Dan. Although I don't even know his real name, I have a strong intuition that he is meant to be part of my destiny. No matter what happens, I'm absolutely certain I shall never forget him.* "I know you're right,

Mama, but how can we find out where he belongs if he can't communicate with us?"

Mama began to unveil her plan. "I've been pondering on this all night," she admitted. "You've got to hitch up the wagon and go into Milltown. You can pick up our supplies while you're there and ask around to see if anyone has heard about a missing person. People in the commissary like to talk a lot. You might hear something that will tell us who he is and where he came from. Don't tell anyone about his being here, though. We sure don't want to start any rumors about us keeping a strange man in our house."

Melissa thought about her mother's plan. It might work, but riding to Milltown and back was close to an all-day affair. She didn't want to leave her mother alone for the second day in a row, especially since now she had added an extra burden. Besides, she had lots of work to do to make up for her absence yesterday.

She usually made the trip to Milltown once or twice a month, taking great care to make a list that would include everything they might need until time to go again. "I can't go today, Mama. I have too much to do. I'll think about it, though, and if Dan isn't any better by tomorrow, maybe I'll go then. That way, you'll have all day to work out our list. I'll go down to the springhouse and see how many eggs I can take with me to barter for our supplies. I'll take along a tub of butter, too."

"But suppose it melts along the way. You know Mr. Whittamore won't buy rancid butter or cracked eggs, either, for that matter. We can't afford to waste our butter and eggs."

"If the weather stays cool like it is today, we shouldn't have to worry about it. I'll wrap it up in wet moss and keep it under the seat, out of the sun. Don't worry, Mama. I'll be careful."

Melissa pushed herself up from the table. "I think I'll

try giving Dan some oatmeal. I'll thin it down with some of this fresh milk and see if I can get him to take it. He needs something that will stick to his ribs and help him get stronger."

"I'll help you," Mama offered. "Don't worry about the dishes. I'll wash them later. You have plenty to do."

Mama followed her daughter into the room where Dan slumbered on. The two women repeated the process of the night before, Mama holding Dan's head while Melissa slipped small amounts of the thin gruel between his lips. Though he spluttered and choked from time to time, Dan swallowed each bite and began to part his lips for more.

"I want to have a look at his wound," Melissa said. With Mama peering over her shoulder, she gently released the bandages covering his chest and lifted the sugar poultice. She searched his chest for red streaks that would indicate blood poisoning. Seeing none, she replaced the dressing and pulled up the muslin sheet to cover his bare arms. His big hands and muscular arms looked almost comical protruding from the sleeves of her father's flannel nightshirt.

Mama took the empty dish to the kitchen, and Melissa turned to follow her. She was almost out the door when she thought she heard his voice.

"Thanks." His word came out in a raspy whisper.

Startled, she whipped around. Had her imagination played tricks on her again? "Dan?" She approached the bed for a closer look. Indeed, his eyes were open and intently focused on her. "You're awake!"

Melissa pulled a straight chair up to the bedside and sat down. She started to ask the question that had plagued her ever since she first laid eyes on him. "Who—"

"Where am I?" His face displayed a mixture of dismay and confusion. "How did I get here?"

"You're with friends," she assured him. She pulled her

chair closer and leaned forward so that she could speak softly. Then slowly and patiently, she began to tell her story from the beginning. "I was out in the woods hunting near the Fenholloway River when I happened to hear a strange noise. I searched the area, trying to locate the source of the cries, and finally found you lying unconscious on the ground. I brought you here to try to save your life."

He furrowed his swollen brow. "How long have I been here?"

"Since yesterday," she told him. "Who are you, and what happened to you?"

For the first time, Melissa saw fear in his eyes. "I don't know," he confessed. "I don't remember anything."

"You've been shot in the shoulder, and you have a nasty bump on your forehead. I think you have a sprained ankle, too. Just give yourself some time. I'm sure you'll be able to remember everything soon." She wished she could feel as confident as she sounded. Seeing his frantic expression as he surveyed his surroundings, she added, "You're not in any danger here. My mother and I will care for you until you're stronger. For now, just try to rest."

As she looked at his swollen, discolored face, Melissa wondered how he could have endured such torture without remembering it. She stood and pushed her chair back against the wall.

"Don't go," he pleaded. "Stay here and talk to me. Please help me remember." Each word came out of his mouth with great effort.

Melissa longed to give him answers that would comfort him and give him peace, but she had nothing to offer. Perhaps by tomorrow he would begin to remember, or maybe someone in Milltown could shed some light on his origin. "I'll be back," she promised.

Periodically throughout the day, she and her mother coaxed

Dan into eating the broth from their venison stew, and they trickled water down his throat to guard against dehydration. Although he continued to show signs of improvement, he still had no answers for their myriad questions. His name and everything about him remained shrouded in mystery.

Melissa spent the day cleaning the little house, washing, and ironing. She made sure Mama would have an adequate supply of water and firewood for the following day. She milked the cow, watered and fed all the animals, and put a big pot of dried beans in a pot to soak overnight.

Melissa brought six nice, big eggs from the springhouse. Added to the six she had gathered that morning, there would be an even dozen to trade. She brought in two tubs of butter, one for the house and one to sell. Packing her goods in a large willow basket, she used Spanish moss from the oak trees to pad everything well. Melissa took great care to wrap each egg separately before she set the basket on the back porch, well away from the heat of the kitchen.

Along with the coins she and Mama had saved from her father's last paycheck, Melissa was sure she'd be able to pay for all their supplies.

At last everything stood in readiness for her journey at daybreak. An exhausted Melissa curled up on the settee beneath her patchwork quilt, and this time she had no difficulty at all in falling into a deep and dreamless sleep.

four

The buckboard bumped along the sandy trail, giving Melissa plenty of time to think about the amazing events of the last two days. She disliked leaving her mother at home alone, but she wasn't concerned for her safety. Not because of Dan's physical weakness, but because she was convinced that he was a good man—she could see kindness written on his face. Mama would be quick to remind her not to judge by outward appearances, but somehow Melissa just knew she wasn't mistaken about Dan. How she knew this, she couldn't have explained if she tried. It was simply a fact, and she was as confident of it as she was of the sun's rising each morning.

Dan had evidently been the victim of foul play. Who could have done such an evil deed? Finding no papers and no money in his possession led Melissa to believe that he might have been attacked by thieves who robbed him and left him for dead.

Suppose she hadn't happened along when she did? She shuddered to imagine his fate. She had found him on the brink of death; surely he could not have lasted much longer. In the surrounding world of nature, Melissa observed that things often seemed to happen for a reason. Was there a reason that brought Dan into her life?

A rumbling sound in the distance startled Dolly. The wagon jerked and veered, almost causing Melissa to lose her balance and fall.

"Whoa, girl," Melissa said, trying to calm the frightened mare. She reined over to the side of the trail and watched. A big freight wagon lumbered by, shaking the ground with its thundering roar. A burly wagoner shouted commands to his oxen team. Huge cypress logs, secured by chains to the flat bed of the wagon, rattled and rumbled like a cage of wild boars. As the gigantic wheels cut deep, ugly ruts into the trail, it took all Melissa's strength to keep Dolly from bolting. She feared for the safety of her eggs, although she had padded them carefully before starting out.

Melissa continued to talk to her horse with soothing tones, trying to calm her enough to continue on her way.

She wondered if the freight wagon belonged to the same company for whom her father worked. Perry Brothers Mills owned many such conveyances, so it could very well be one of theirs. She wondered anew when her father would return home. He might have even helped fell the mighty trees that just passed by.

Rumor had it that many of the cypress trees had been cut from some sections of the tidewater swamp. It took hundreds of years to grow those magnificent trees, so the lumber companies frequently moved their workforces to different locales where timber was more plentiful. Maybe Papa would soon be working closer to home, but then again, he might be sent even farther away.

The Perry Brothers Mills operated Milltown. Their commissary carried all the anticipated supplies needed by their employees and their families. Customers were allowed to sign a tab for their purchases when money was scarce and have the amount deducted from their paychecks at the end of the pay period. But Papa preferred for his family to pay in cash, and Melissa and Mama tried to respect his wishes. By doing business that way, on payday the full amount would belong to them.

Bartering was a way of life for the pioneer families. Everything from farm produce to handmade clothing could be exchanged for food and needed supplies. Melissa and Mama always gathered up whatever surpluses they had and took them to the commissary for barter.

On normal occasions, Melissa always enjoyed these shopping trips. When time permitted, she could browse through *Godey's Lady's Book* to check out the latest fashions and hairstyles. She liked to run her fingers over the bolts of new fabric, imagining what creations her mother could turn out if given the chance.

She especially enjoyed milling around the store, visiting with friends, and catching up on all the local news. She had a special purpose for wanting to hear news this day. Would she hear something to shed light on the mysterious Dan?

Because Dolly still seemed nervous, Melissa decided she should hitch her to a tree and stop to eat some of the corn bread and oranges she had brought along for lunch. Then she had another idea. She calculated that she wasn't far from the Taylor ranch. She hadn't seen her friend Josie Ann since the Christmas frolic in Mr. Taylor's barn. It wouldn't be much out of her way, and maybe Josie Ann would ride the rest of the way into Milltown with her.

She had a hard time weaving the bulky old wagon between the trees, but Dolly seemed happy to leave the trail in favor of the sheltering forest. Travel was much slower than when riding along the trail, and Melissa began to wonder if she had made a mistake in coming this way. Just as she was beginning to despair, she came into the familiar clearing that led up to the Taylor home.

Josie Ann squealed with delight when she saw her friend. "Melissa, I'm so glad you've come. I've so much to tell you." She dragged her through the doorway and into the spacious kitchen. "We're just fixin' to sit down to dinner. Mattie, set an extra place for Melissa," she called to the maid.

Mrs. Taylor gave Melissa a warm hug. "By all means, honey. Come sit a spell and tell us all about your family."

At the mention of the noon meal, Melissa's cheeks flamed in embarrassment. She should have realized she was stopping at their dinner hour. "Please forgive me for stopping in at dinnertime. I'm on my way to Milltown for supplies, and I wanted to see if Josie Ann would ride in with me."

"Nonsense, child. We're plumb delighted you're here. Mr. Taylor won't be home until suppertime. He's out with the cow hunters because they're branding today, so it's just me and Josie Ann. We're happy for the company. Is your daddy back home yet?"

"No, ma'am. We're expecting him most any day." Melissa remembered her mother's warning about not mentioning Dan to anyone. It would be difficult to carry on a conversation with her close friend without confiding the thoughts uppermost in her mind, but she'd have to keep a tight lock on her lips and try to avoid a slipup.

"And how is Doralee feeling these days?"

"Mama's much better, thank you." Melissa allowed them to usher her into the dining room, where a big noonday meal was spread across the table.

"Sit here by me," Josie Ann begged. "After dinner I want to show you the bedspread I'm crocheting for my hope chest." Her eyes sparkled mysteriously.

Melissa wasn't surprised. She had seen Josie Ann and her beau whispering and holding hands at the Christmas frolic. She'd figured it was only a matter of time before she'd be invited to a wedding. "Tell me all about it, Josie Ann."

Josie Ann needed no encouragement. "Come on then. Dinner can wait a few minutes." She dragged her friend up the staircase to her room. "This is what I'm working on." She spread her crocheting across the bed for Melissa's inspection.

"It's going to be beautiful!"

"I got the instructions out of the newest issue of *Ladies Magazine*. Here, I've saved some of my old copies for you."

Josie Ann gave her two back issues of the popular publication. Then she pulled from beneath her bed a well-worn copy of *Graham's Magazine.* "Take this one, too. It has some juicy love stories in it." Josie Ann giggled. "You better keep this one out of sight. Your mama might not approve of some of those stories, but I find them very exciting."

Melissa loved books and magazines, and Josie Ann was always generous about sharing hers. When Melissa had been just a little girl, Mama had taught her to read from some old readers she had stashed away in her trunk. Since that time, Melissa had devoured every book she could get her hands on.

"Thanks, Josie Ann. You know how much I enjoy these." The two girls descended the staircase hand in hand.

During the meal, Melissa heard all about Hank's superior attributes: his strong physique, his adorable smile, and his skill with a rifle. "We're looking to early summer for the wedding. The circuit rider should be coming this way in May or June."

Finally Mrs. Taylor broke in. "That's enough, Josie Ann. You haven't given Melissa a chance to get a word in edgewise, and I want to hear all about what's going on over their way."

"Um, not much," Melissa hedged. *Be careful not to mention Dan.* "That influenza hit Mama mighty hard this winter, and she's still pretty weak. She can't do a lot without stopping to rest."

"So then, it's just the two of you now, right?"

Why did Mrs. Taylor have to phrase her question like that? Did Melissa only imagine that her hostess's eyes seemed to pierce right into her head, almost as though she could read some unusual piece of news?

She felt the blood rising to her cheeks. She didn't want to tell a fib, but neither did she want to admit there were three of them now instead of two. Hoping her confusion went unnoticed, she changed the subject. "Josie Ann, do you want to ride into town with me? I hate to eat and run, but I need to get back home in time to milk Flossie tonight."

"I'd better not," Josie Ann demurred. "I think Hank is going to stop in after he gets done branding. But I'll walk you out to the gate."

Melissa blotted her lips with her napkin. "Thank you for a delicious dinner, Mrs. Taylor. If I may be excused. . ."

"Of course, dear. Try to come again soon, and next time bring your mama." She pushed away from the table. "Hold up just a minute, Melissa. I want to send Doralee a loaf of my fresh-baked pumpkin bread."

While she was out of the room, Josie Ann clasped Melissa's hands. "I want you to help me plan my wedding. Can you ride over on Sunday so we can talk about it? You could spend the night, and we could talk all night long, like we used to do when we were younger."

Melissa couldn't make any plans as long as she had Dan to worry about, but of course she couldn't explain that to her friend. "Um, no, I think I'd better stay close to home until Mama is stronger, but thanks for inviting me." She edged toward the door, conscious of the blush spreading over her face.

"Of course," Josie Ann agreed. "How thoughtless of me. I know what we can do. I'll just ride over to your house, and we can both spend the day helping your mother. How's that?" She bounced with enthusiasm.

"Yes—I mean, no. I can't let you do that."

"Why not? Melissa, you're not acting like yourself today. I know you have a lot on your shoulders, what with your daddy being gone and all and your mother not feeling well. I'd really like to come over and help. It's the least I could do for my best friend."

I should never have stopped here. How am I going to get out of this mess? I'm no good at deception. Melissa gave Josie Ann a tight hug. "You're a true friend, but you mustn't come this week. I. . .um. . .my father may be coming home, and you know how men are. They like to have the house quiet and all."

"Of course." Josie Ann backed away, obviously miffed by Melissa's lack of appreciation for her generous offer. "Well, thank you for stopping by."

"And thank *you* for a wonderful dinner and for the magazines, too." She hadn't meant to hurt Josie Ann's feelings. She gave her another quick hug and kissed her on the cheek.

Melissa was spared further embarrassment when Mrs. Taylor bore down on her with a wicker basket covered with a red-checkered cloth. "Now you take this home to your mama, and tell her I hope she's able to come with you on your next trip to Milltown." She kissed Melissa on the forehead and gave a gentle push to her back. "Now scoot, so you can get your shopping done and get home before dark."

❧

When Melissa entered the commissary, her first obligation was to deliver her eggs and butter to Mr. Whittamore for his inspection.

"Well now, that's mighty nice, Miss Malcolm." The old storekeeper carefully unwrapped each egg and lifted the tub of butter from her basket. "Folks around here always tell me your butter is sweeter than all the others, and these eggs look nice and fresh." He took a stub of a pencil from behind his ear and made notations in his book. "You go ahead and look around. I'll just put this stuff in the cool box, and we'll figure everything out later, after you decide what you want."

Melissa walked around collecting the items she needed, stopping to chat with a few of the people she recognized. She looked at Mr. Whittamore's bulletin board to see if he had posted any important announcements. She read the notes with interest.

She smiled at two offers of matrimony crudely written in pencil by loggers evidently lonely for home-cooked meals and female companionship.

Then another notice caught her eye. WANTED. ARMED AND DANGEROUS. The poster described a recent robbery right in the commissary. A bandit brandishing a pistol had demanded all the money from Mr. Whittamore's cashbox, then rode away. Melissa thought about her long ride home and hoped she would not encounter the dangerous outlaw.

At last her shopping was complete, but she had not accomplished the main mission for which she came. She put her purchases on the wooden counter for Mr. Whittamore's inspection. Out came his notebook and pencil, and the grocer began his ciphering. After he added up both sides of the page, one for her purchases and the other for the value of her butter and eggs, he turned the paper around so that Melissa could check his figures. "Comes to one dollar and two bits you owe me, Miss Malcolm. Shall I just put that on a tab for you?"

Melissa opened her leather drawstring purse and carefully counted out her coins. "No thank you, Mr. Whittamore. I prefer to pay."

"Well, we thank ye kindly," he said, scooping up the money from the counter. "Just remember, your credit is always good at the commissary."

Melissa stalled, wondering how she could get some revealing information. "Um, what's been going on around here lately, Mr. Whittamore? Any weddings, new babies, um, you know—anything I can go home and tell Mama about? She's always hungry to hear all the local news."

The old man scratched his head. "Well now, let's see. Mrs. Simpson has a new set of twins. Two little boys. Named them Joshua and Jeremiah. Course, the really big news was our robbery last week. I reckon you heard about that."

"Yes, I read about that on your wanted poster. Tell me what happened." This was not the news she came to hear about, but maybe if he kept talking, he would remember a family reporting a missing person.

"Well, it was a mighty unnerving experience, I'll tell you. This young whippersnapper barged in here demanding cash. Looking right into the barrel of that rifle, I couldn't do nothing but give him everything I had. He took off on his horse and headed north. The sheriff sent out a posse to follow him, and they almost caught up with him. One of the deputies was sure he landed a shot in the man's right shoulder, but the scoundrel kept on riding until he was clean out of sight. No one's seen hide nor hair of him since, and I'm still out near 'bout two hundred dollars. You better be careful riding through those woods, Miss Malcolm."

"I will," she said. *It couldn't have been Dan because he didn't have a horse, much less a gun and stolen money.* "What did he look like, Mr. Whittamore?"

"Well, I got a good look at him. I'll never forget that face. He was a big man with kinda yellow hair."

Melissa felt faint. *It just couldn't be!* "Do you remember the color of his eyes?"

Mr. Whittamore scratched his head again, trying to recall. "They was light, either blue or green—maybe gray. Leastways, I know they weren't brown."

Melissa put both hands on the counter to keep her balance. Her head began to reel.

"Are you all right, Miss Malcolm? I'm afeared I scared you talking about that bandit. Now don't you worry your head about it. The sheriff has got his men out looking. Just you try to get home before dark."

"Yes. Yes, I must do that." Melissa put her smaller purchases in her basket. "Could someone put this sack of feed in the back of my wagon?"

"Yes, miss. Jonah?" Mr. Whittamore called to a young clerk, and by the time Melissa climbed up in her wagon, the feed and all her other purchases were stashed in the bed of her buckboard.

five

The last remnants of daylight were waning by the time Melissa drove her wagon into the barn.

She unhitched Dolly and rewarded the old mare's efforts with a generous scoop of grain. "Good girl!" She lifted her basket out of the wagon and had just started across the yard to the house when she noticed a man's jacket hanging from the clothesline. She knew that jacket, and it could mean only one thing!

"Papa's home!" Melissa broke into a run and fairly flew up the back steps. The rest of her supplies could wait until later. Oh, joy! Papa was so smart. He'd think of some way to help them find information about Dan.

Melissa was now more convinced than ever that Dan's presence must remain a secret. After what she had learned today, it was possible someone might try to link his identity to the commissary robbery. In her heart, Melissa knew Dan was not capable of such an act, but would others believe as she did?

She could hear her parents engaged in heated conversation in the parlor. Why would they argue on the eve of Papa's return? This was supposed to be a happy time. She rushed into the parlor and threw her arms wide in anticipation of Papa's embrace, but instead he looked at her with cold eyes. "Melissa, are you out of your mind?"

"Oh, Papa, I'm so glad you're home. Mama and I have so much to tell you." Her beloved father was home! She tried to wrap her arms around him, but he put his hands on her shoulders and held her back, looking into her face with angry eyes.

"If you're talking about this foolhardy act of bringing a stranger home with you, I've already been told. I thought better of you, Melissa. I depend on you to take care of things here while I'm away. Whatever possessed you to do such a dangerous thing?"

"But, Papa. . ." Melissa's words ended in a big sob, and for a moment she couldn't continue. She had been so certain her father would understand. He was the one who always sided with her when she brought home injured stray animals and nursed them back to health. He had a heart filled with kindness and generosity. Surely she could make him understand how important this was to her. She tried again. "I found him near Daniel Creek, up by the Fenholloway River. There was no one else around to help him, and I could see he was near death. Papa, you wouldn't have gone off and left him in the woods to die alone, would you? I know you wouldn't have."

Her father loosened his grip on her shoulders and drew her into his embrace. "You're right, Melissa. I wouldn't have. But I'm a man, and that makes all the difference in the world."

"I don't see why," Melissa protested. "When it comes to saving a man's life, I don't see what difference it makes whether you're—"

"Of course you don't see because you're just an innocent young girl. I know you meant well, honey, but by bringing this man into our home, you've put yourself and your mama in a very dangerous position."

Melissa knew from experience that it seldom paid to argue with her father, especially when he was hungry and tired. Perhaps things would go more smoothly if she could approach him with her arguments on a full stomach. Instead of responding to his last remark, she turned to her mother. "What's that I smell? Are you making another pot of that delicious venison stew like we had last night?"

Mama beamed. "Yes, and I've made a special salad with carrots and orange sections. It has pecans and whipped cream in it, too. We're going to turn your father's homecoming into a party." She slipped into the kitchen, and Melissa turned to follow her.

"You needn't think this matter is over, Melissa," her father called after her. "We'll get this thing resolved before I leave tomorrow."

Melissa stopped dead in her tracks. "Tomorrow? But, Papa, you just got here."

"We'll talk about this later. Go to the kitchen and help your mother now. I'm going out to the pump to wash up before supper."

Melissa had refrained from asking her mother about Dan, not wanting to fan the flames of her father's ire. But she simply couldn't wait another minute to ask. As soon as she heard the back door slam, she lowered her voice to a whisper. "Mama, how is Dan?"

"He's doing good, honey, but his talking still doesn't make much sense. I brought his clothes in off the line and ironed them. He seemed happy to change out of your papa's nightshirt. I took him his dinner at noon, and he cleaned his plate. He's been sleeping ever since. Your father got home only a few minutes ahead of you, so he hasn't seen him yet, but he was fit to be tied when I told him."

"Mama, you've got to help me persuade Papa to let us keep Dan until he's stronger. We can't turn this poor, sick man out into the woods. He would surely die before morning."

"I don't know, Melissa. I'm not sure anymore about what's the right thing to do." Mama used a pot holder to lift the lid to her stew pot and gave the contents a stir with her big wooden spoon.

"I'll be right back, Mama." Taking advantage of her father's absence from the house, Melissa ran to her bedroom to check on Dan. Her breath came rapidly as she approached the closed door. She knocked lightly before she entered.

Dan tried to raise his head from the pillow, and Melissa saw that it took great effort. He was still very weak, but he looked pleased to see her. "You're back." He shifted his body beneath the covers and smiled at her. His incredible smile worked its magic on her, leaving her knees as weak as wet newspaper.

Melissa crossed the room on shaking legs and stood next to his bed. "Yes. I didn't want to go off and leave Mama on her own today, but I had to go to the commissary to, um, to get some supplies." She didn't want to reveal her real reason for leaving today. "Mama told me you ate a good dinner. Are you feeling stronger?"

"Yes, much. I think I'll be up and out of here before long. You and your ma have been very kind to me."

Melissa's heart plummeted. *Did he say "out of here?"* "Where will you go?"

Once again, a puzzled look blanketed his face. He shook his head and furrowed his brow. "I honestly don't know. I've been trying all day to remember, but no matter how hard I try, I can't recall who I am or where I came from."

Reading the deep concern in his eyes, Melissa tried to comfort him. "Don't worry about it now, Dan. Your body has suffered a great shock. Once you've fully recovered from your accident, I'm sure your memory will return. Give it some time." Melissa wished she felt as sure of that as she tried to sound.

His head jerked upward. "You called me 'Dan.' Is that my name? How did you learn my name?"

Melissa could feel the flush rising to her cheeks. "It's just a name I gave you myself," she confessed. "I needed something to call you until we find out your true identity."

His lips curved in a sweet, half smile, and he reached out

and touched her arm. "You're unbelievable. A real-life angel."

The touch of his hand on her flesh sent a tingling sensation up her arm. How had Dan come to be so important to her in such a short time?

Melissa was reluctant to leave his side, but she didn't want to risk her father's wrath. He would be coming back inside for supper at any minute, and if he didn't find her in the kitchen, he would likely come looking for her. She mustn't do anything to vex him when so much hung in the balance.

She touched Dan's forehead with the tips of her fingers, justifying the action by telling herself she needed to check on his temperature. His flesh felt cool and soft against her hand. "I have to go now, but I'll come back. I'll bring you a supper tray later."

She had already lingered longer than she intended. Papa would soon be done with his bath, and he would be furious if he found her talking to Dan. She slipped out of the room and hurried to help her mother in the kitchen.

Melissa set the oak sawbuck table with eating utensils and three blue enamel plates, while Mama stoked up the fire in the stove. Mama filled a pan with water from her jug and set it on the burner to heat. Then she picked up two pot holders and used them to remove hot biscuits from the oven, placing the pan of hot bread in the warming oven atop the stove.

"Melissa, run back to the springhouse and bring up some of that nice, thick cream for your papa's coffee. Hurry now, before it gets pitch dark."

Glad to be outside in the cool evening air, Melissa did as she was told. Overhead, stars twinkled in the heavens, and a crescent moon hung over the little house. Everything seemed better when Papa was home. If only she could make him understand about Dan. One look into his amazing blue eyes should be enough to convince Papa he was not a dangerous man.

In her haste to get back into the kitchen ahead of her father, she almost tripped over their old hound dog, who lay on the back steps, gnawing on a bone. She put the cream on the table. "There you are, Mama."

A few minutes later, Papa came in through the back door, whistling. "It's mighty nice to come back home to my two best girls." He cast a satisfied glance at the pot of stew and sniffed the fragrant air. "I sure do miss this kind of cooking when I'm living in the logging camp. We don't ever get anything that smells like this." He gave his wife a hug and pecked her on the cheek.

"Get on with you now." Mama pushed him aside, but her rosy blush revealed her pleasure in her husband's attentions.

Supper was almost ready when Melissa remembered her basket of supplies. In her haste to see Papa, she had come into the house and deposited it on the sideboard. In all the excitement, she had not thought about it since. "I stopped by the Taylor ranch on the way to the commissary. Mrs. Taylor sent you her best wishes, Mama, and some of her pumpkin bread."

"Now, wasn't that nice," Mama exclaimed. "Slice some of it, Daughter, and put it on the table. That'll be mighty tasty with our stew."

During supper, no mention was made of the stranger in the bedroom, but Melissa did not delude herself into thinking the matter was over. Hoping to maintain the cheerful atmosphere, she regaled her parents with an account of her day, even telling about the ox-driven load of cypress that had spooked Dolly and forced them off the trail. But she thought it best not to mention the blond outlaw who had held up the commissary.

"And how is Josie Ann?" Mama asked. "I know she was happy to see you."

Melissa grinned. "Josie Ann is in love. She's planning on getting married this summer. That's all she could talk about."

Papa speared a piece of venison with his fork and suspended it in midair. "I'd say it's about time. Isn't she about twenty, like you, Melissa?"

Melissa's cheeks burned. She sensed the direction this conversation was headed and wished she could think of some way to reroute it. "Um, yes, sir. I think we're about the same age."

"Well, now, that's mighty nice that she's getting married," Papa continued. "I know her folks are proud. And while we're on the subject of weddings. . ."

Oh, here it comes!

"How's that fine Mr. Blake getting along these days?" He winked at his wife. "Last time I saw him, he seemed mighty anxious to pay court to my pretty daughter. I gave him my permission, of course. He's one of the most successful ranchers in the area, and if you play your cards right, Melissa, you could soon—"

"Papa, *please.* I hardly know Mr. Blake."

"He *is* a real charmer," Mama agreed. "Why, he's the one responsible for this delicious venison we're having for supper tonight."

Melissa squirmed in her chair. If only she could think of some reason to excuse herself from the table. She fixed her eyes on her bowl and continued to eat, although her appetite had suddenly disappeared. She tried to divert the conversation.

"Mr. Whittamore said the Simpsons have a new set of twins. Joshua and Jeremiah, I believe he said."

"Land sakes," Mama wailed. "I think that makes seven mouths for the Simpsons to feed. I don't know how they do it."

Papa smiled broadly. "Well, at least that's one thing you and Melissa won't have to worry about anytime soon." He dug in his pockets and pulled out a worn leather pouch. He untied the drawstrings and released a stash of gold and silver coins. They made a delightful clink as he dropped them on the table. "This should hold you over until I get home again, with a little extra to spare. There's enough there for you two ladies to buy some cloth at the commissary and make yourselves something pretty to wear."

Mama clapped her hands in delight. "Did you hear that, Melissa? We can pick out a pretty new voile print to make dresses for Josie Ann's wedding." She rose from the table and fetched their money box from the top shelf of the cupboard. She counted the coins as she deposited them in the small wooden chest. "Why, Cleve, how did you ever manage to bring home so much this time?"

Papa leaned back in his chair and puffed out his chest. "We've been working from daylight to dark, and there's nothing to spend it on out there in the tidewater swamp. The crew leader paid us all in cash just before he sent us home. Some of the fellows headed straight for the taverns, but most of them are like me, with family at home waiting for them."

Melissa began to clear the table, while her father regaled them with news he had picked up from the logging camp. "Florida may soon become a state," he told them, "although progress is slow because the delegates can't agree over whether the capital should be located in Pensacola to the west or St. Augustine in the east. They've set up voting places in the territory to determine the people's wishes, but there's been a lot of corruption by fellows who change things to suit their own purposes."

Melissa poured hot water into her dishpan and reached for a bar of lye soap. "How can they change a vote, Papa?"

"Easy. When a man marks an X by his choice, his mark can be erased by some scalawag vote counter. There's talk of doing it a better way by using some kind of newfangled punch cards. To vote, you'd simply punch a hole in a card next to your choice. If they could get that system in place, there couldn't be any more question about the votes."

Mama picked up a tea towel to help with the dishes, but Melissa laid a soapy hand on her arm. "I'll finish up in here, Mama. You just go in the parlor and visit with Papa." She didn't want to fix Dan's tray while her father watched. It would only stir up more questions.

"Papa's tired," her mother said. "I expect he'll be wanting to get to bed before long."

"Not before I get a few things settled," Papa said, rising from the table. "I'll wait in the parlor until you're finished with the dishes, Melissa. Hurry it up, though. Your mama's right—I am tired. My own bed is gonna feel mighty good tonight."

"Yes, Papa." Melissa plunged her hands into the hot water and began to scrub the plates with a vengeance. What could she possibly say to soften her father's heart? Dan was already talking about leaving, so what harm would come in having him stay a few more days? Melissa used her dishrag to wipe the tabletop, stalling for a few more minutes before facing Papa with what was sure to be an uncomfortable confrontation. The problem wasn't going to resolve itself. She might as well just go ahead and get it over with.

six

Mama stood apart from them, letting her husband handle the difficult situation. Papa led his daughter to the settee. "Sit here by me, darlin', and let's talk about this in a sensible manner."

Melissa took her place beside him, determined to do battle for her cause. She seldom went against his wishes about anything, but this was too important to give up easily. She held his big, rough hands in her own and tried to reach him on his most vulnerable issues.

"Papa, you have such a kind heart. You've never turned a hungry person away from our door. Why, I've seen how much it hurts you to kill an innocent deer, even when we need food on the table. I just know you couldn't turn your back on a person with a real need."

The kind man looked into his daughter's eyes with such tenderness that Melissa felt for a moment she had driven her point home. Reaping courage from his hesitancy, she plunged forward. "It's only for a short time, until he gets strong enough to take care of himself in the woods. He's getting better every day."

Papa shook his head. "If I could stay here to take care of you, there'd be no question about helping this poor man. But with you and your mama here alone, I just don't feel it's safe."

Melissa tried a new argument. "What harm could he possibly do? Think about it. He has no gun, and he's as weak as a baby kitten."

Her hopes soared when her father scratched his head and

turned to look at his wife. "What do you think about all this, Doralee?"

Melissa sent her mother a pleading look. Mama shifted her gaze from her husband to her daughter and back again. "He. . .he isn't much trouble, Cleve, and he does seem to appreciate the little we've done for him."

Papa stood up and began to pace back and forth in the small room. Melissa held her breath. She could see him wrestling with his decision.

"Supposing—now, I just said 'supposing' because I haven't reached a decision yet—but supposing I did say he could stay around for a few days. I'd have some stipulations."

"Anything, Papa. We'll do anything you say."

"Well, first off, I've been thinking about leaving my rifle here in case y'all had need of it, but with this stranger on the property, we'd have to think of a good place to hide it out of sight."

"We could put it in the bottom of my trunk," Mama offered. "No one would ever think to look there for a gun."

"Or how about that box in the back of the wagon? I could cover it up with an old quilt, and no one would recognize it, even if they did happen to see it. That way I'd have it with me whenever we ride to the commissary."

Melissa scarcely dared to breathe while she watched her father roll the idea around in his mind.

After a long pause, he said, "That might not be such a bad idea. You think you can handle that thing, Melissa?"

"Yes, Papa. You took me out in the woods and taught me how to use it when I was ten years old. But what about you? Won't you need it for protection?"

Papa shook his head. "Nearly every man in our outfit has a gun of some kind. Anyway, nobody ever messes with the logging crews. Who'd have the nerve to confront a big group of strong men equipped with axes and saws? I'll leave the rifle here with y'all this time. It'll be one less thing I'll have to carry, and I'll feel better knowing you have the extra protection."

Melissa's hopes soared until she heard her father's next words. "I still don't like the idea of having that man under the same roof with my womenfolk. He could attack you in your sleep, and I wouldn't hear about it until I came home again. No, I'm sorry, but I absolutely cannot permit him to stay in this house."

So he *was* going to make them turn him out after all! Salty tears pooled in Melissa's eyes until another idea entered her mind. "What if we make him a place in the barn? We could take food to him and give him a blanket to keep warm on cool nights. At least he'd have shelter from the wind and rain. Could we do that, Papa?"

Papa rubbed his chin, a sure sign he was thinking. "Well, I don't know. Suppose he took it into his head to steal our horse and leave? What could you do about that?"

Melissa knew in her heart that Dan would never do such a thing, but she'd have to come up with a better reason than that. "In the first place, he'd never be able to mount a horse. Even if he did, poor old Dolly is so slow, he couldn't get very far. Oh, Papa, let's just trust him a little bit. He needs help so badly."

Melissa knew she had won when he said, "I'll have to sleep on it. I'll decide in the morning. But bring the lamp, and I'll take him out to the barn tonight. He's not staying inside here another night."

Fear gripped Melissa like a vise. How long could Dan, in his weakened condition, survive in the barn? But she knew better than to press her father for more privileges. "I'll help you move him, Papa. He's too heavy for you to lift alone."

She led the way into her bedroom, where Dan lay sleeping beneath her patchwork quilt. Startled by their footsteps, his eyelids flew open, and his expression revealed apprehension.

Melissa didn't want to disturb him, but she knew she had no choice. "This is my father," she began. "I'm sorry, but we're going to move you out to the barn tonight. I'll fix you a bed of hay in the tack room and give you a blanket to help you keep warm."

Dan raised his head from the pillow. "That's fine. I've been a great deal of trouble to y'all for much too long." He struggled to a sitting position and slid his legs over the edge of the bed.

Up until now, although her father hadn't spoken a word, Melissa was encouraged by the expression of pity on his face. She had seen that same expression before, whenever he treated a wounded animal or fed a hungry stranger. Her papa was a kind man!

"Here, let me help you, young fellow." Papa sat beside him on the bed and pulled Dan's arm around his neck. Together they raised Dan to his feet.

"Lean on me, too," Melissa said, positioning herself on his opposite side. He put a hand on her shoulder, but his bandages and his wound prevented him from raising his arm any higher. With Dan shuffling between them, Melissa and her father inched slowly through the house to the back door, where Mama carried a lantern and held the door open for them.

Half an hour later, the little group stood in the light of the whale-oil lantern and eased Dan onto a mound of clean hay. The injured man stifled a groan as Melissa slipped a pillow beneath his head and covered him with a blanket. Her heart ached to see him suffer that way. She would gladly have sacrificed her own bed for as long as it took, but she knew better than to suggest it. She didn't want to upset Papa and lose the small victory she had gained tonight.

The effort of moving to the barn had completely exhausted Dan, and he was already asleep again. If the hay was scratchy and uncomfortable, he gave no sign of it. Melissa regretted that she hadn't even given him his supper, but at this point, he seemed to need rest more than food. With a heavy heart, she led the way back to the house, and Papa followed.

⋟

Before the break of day, Papa lit the lantern and sat at the kitchen table with Mama beside him, while Melissa cooked breakfast.

"I wish you didn't have to go away again so soon, Papa. Will you be gone very long this time?"

Over a plate of fried eggs and grits, he shook his head. "There's no way of knowing, honey. We're heading for the Georgia line, up in the Okefenokee Swamp. That'll be rough living for a while, but the pay's good."

"Just be careful," his wife warned him. "I know there's all kinds of danger in those swamps."

Papa smiled. He slathered butter on one of last night's biscuits. "You don't need to worry about me. I know how to take care of myself. It's you two who need to be careful, what with that stranger out there in the barn. I'm still a mite uneasy about that." He added guava jelly to his biscuit. "Just get him on his way as soon as you can."

"We will," Mama promised, but Melissa remained silent.

"There's another thing I want to talk about," Papa said, stirring a tablespoon of molasses into his coffee. "Harrison Blake is a big man in these parts. He's got a two-thousand-acre spread and a fine house. About the only thing he doesn't have is a wife. A girl could do a lot worse." He gave Melissa a meaningful glance.

"I–I'm not looking to get married, Papa."

"Be sensible, Daughter. Your mother and I won't always be around to take care of you, and you're not getting any younger. It's time you began to think about settling down with a good man who can provide for you. It's not as though you'll have lots of choices, like as though you was in the States. Out here in the Florida Territory, prosperous gentlemen are few and far between."

"But I'm not fond of Harrison Blake, Papa. When I get married, I want to fall madly in love like Josie Ann." Melissa gazed dreamily out of the kitchen window.

"Hogwash!" her father exclaimed. "You've been wasting too much of your time reading those ladies' magazines Josie Ann gives you. That kind of foolishness will lead to trouble. I've already told Mr. Blake he could call on you, Melissa, and I want you to be nice to him."

"I will, Papa. I'll be nice to him."

"Good. Next time I come home, I won't be surprised if there's a wedding in your plans." He looked down at his plate, and Melissa was relieved that he did not see her involuntary shudder. He looked as pleased as though he had already given away his daughter in matrimony. He used an unbleached muslin napkin to wipe his lips and rose from the table. "I'm going out back to wash up. I'll look in on that feller in the barn to make sure my horse is still there."

"Oh, Papa, shame on you. Dan's never given us any reason to believe he's anything but a gentleman. Wait, and I'll dish up some grits and eggs for you to give him." She scooped a mound of grits from the kettle and topped it with a scrambled egg. Adding a buttered biscuit to the plate, she handed it to her father. "This should stick to his ribs." She added a pitcher of water and a tin cup. "Can you carry all this, or do you need some help?"

"I can manage," her father assured her, hooking the cup on his little finger as he lifted the plate and pitcher with his two big hands.

Melissa was secretly disappointed. She had hoped to be the one to take Dan his breakfast. But maybe if Papa had a chance to know Dan better, he'd see he wasn't a horse thief.

Melissa was washing dishes when Papa came back inside with his towel and an empty plate. "He ate every last bite." He dropped the plate into the dishpan of sudsy water.

"The coffee's still hot," Mama told him. "Don't you want another cup before you leave?"

"I reckon I'd better get started. I've got a good hour of walking ahead of me. Our work gang is meeting at the fork in the trail where it branches off east toward Tallahassee. The logging truck is picking us up there before we head northwest toward the Georgia boundary and the Okefenokee Swamp."

Mama wiped her hands on her apron. "I hate to see you go, Cleve. It's been awful nice having you home, but it just wasn't long enough."

"I wish I could stay here long enough to put in our spring garden. When summer comes, I'm going to try to find work closer to home," he promised her. "Maybe I can get hired on at that sawmill over near Milltown." He kissed his wife, picked up his bulging knapsack, and headed toward the backyard.

Melissa followed him, carrying a croker sack. "Here's some grub for your trip, Papa. Please take care of yourself, and hurry home. We'll miss you."

A loud bellow from the barn was Flossie's reminder that she hadn't been milked yet. "Hush, Flossie. I'll get to you in a few minutes, after I give Papa a send-off," Melissa hollered in reply.

Papa gave his only daughter a kiss on the cheek. "I'll miss you, too, honey." He changed his battered old suitcase to his left hand and grabbed the sack of food with his right. "Take good care of your mama, and don't forget all those things you promised me."

"I won't, Papa." With tears stinging the backs of her eyelids, Melissa waved to him until he was out of sight.

seven

Before beginning her multitude of morning chores, Melissa rapped gently on the tack-room door and opened it just enough to slip through. "I'm sorry you had to sleep out here last night," she apologized, stepping over a pitchfork to enter the small cubicle. "Did you have enough breakfast? We still have grits in the kettle."

"I'm fine, getting stronger by the minute," Dan said, rising on his good arm and smiling at her. "Your father came out here and had a little talk with me before he left this morning."

Melissa's eyes clouded. "I hope he wasn't unkind to you."

"He was nice, but I could tell he's worried. I can't blame him for being concerned for his family. He doesn't know anything at all about me, and I couldn't even tell him my name, no matter how much I wanted to. He just wants to take care of you and your ma, and I certainly can't fault him for that."

Melissa sat on an overturned nail keg. "It must be very troubling not remembering who you are or where you live. Is anything coming back in your memory? Anything at all?"

Dan furrowed his brow. "Every now and then, I get a little flash of something. Like when the cow bellowed this morning. That was a familiar sound. I know I'm used to cows and horses. And what is Tallahassee? I seem to remember something by that name."

"Tallahassee is a couple of days northwest of here. Perhaps that's where you came from, but why in the world would you be way over here in this area? There's nothing around here but a few poor dirt farmers and a couple of big cattle ranches. Do you think you might have been looking for work?"

"Maybe. I just can't seem to remember. It's very frustrating. One day soon I'll be able to put it all together, though. I know I was riding a horse, and it seems like I had something heavy in my saddlebags."

"But there was no horse anywhere near," Melissa reminded him. "You were just out in the woods alone. No gun, no horse—nothing. If you did come from Tallahassee, you sure couldn't have walked this far, so maybe you did indeed ride a horse. Whoever put that bullet through your shoulder must have taken off with your horse and whatever you carried in your saddlebags."

Dan shook his head in frustration. "I'll keep trying to remember. I'm sure it will all come to me soon. One thing I remember is that I like to read. Do you have any books in your house that I could borrow?"

Melissa didn't want to tell him about the ladies' magazines Josie Ann gave her from time to time. She hardly thought he would want to learn about the latest women's fashions. She avoided answering his question by asking one of her own. "What kind of books do you like?"

"If you'd trust me with it, I'd like to use your Bible. Would you mind if I read it out here? I'd take care not to let it get soiled."

"Our Bible?" Of all the books he might have requested, she would never have thought of a Bible. She had seen one at Josie Ann's house, but her parents didn't have one. "I'm sorry," she admitted. "We don't have a Bible, but I'll see what else I can find. I think we have some old copies of *The Saturday Evening Post*. Do you like that?"

He frowned, trying to remember. "That sounds familiar. Maybe if I saw it, I might start to recollect something. I just thought—you're sure you don't have a Bible?"

"Quite sure, but my father has a few old books. I'll see what I can find. And I'll fill up your water pitcher and bring it back to you. Is there anything else you can think of to make you more comfortable?"

"Not unless you want to stay out here and talk to me. I know you have plenty of work to do, but you sure are a sight to look at." Observing Melissa's blush, he was quick to add, "I'm sorry if I sounded too forward. The words in my head just popped out."

Melissa was not accustomed to such compliments from gentlemen. She was sure she must look a mess after standing over the woodstove for the last hour. Her hands flew to her hair. She took a moment to regain her composure. "I took no offense, Dan, and I thank you kindly." She stooped over and picked up his water pitcher. "I'll bring this back in a few minutes, and I'll get Mama to help me put a clean dressing on your shoulder. I'll look for some books, too."

At the door, she turned and looked back over her shoulder for one last glance at this strange man who had suddenly come to mean so much to her. For a brief moment, their gazes locked, and the current that passed between them transcended words. In a state of confusion, Melissa turned and scurried across the yard to her house.

⋙

Mama straightened the sheets on her bed, and Melissa helped her cover them with one of her patchwork quilts.

"I put the fresh milk in the springhouse. Flossie was right generous today. I'll make some butter after a bit."

"You're a good girl, Melissa. What would I ever do without you?"

"I'm going to need some help when I change Dan's dressing today, Mama. Let's take care of it right after dinner. It's harder to take care of him in the barn than when he was in the house."

"I reckon we can do that anytime you're ready," Mama said. "Have you talked to him this morning?"

"Yes, and that reminds me. I need to take him some of Papa's books and magazines. He said he would like to have something to read."

Mama pulled some old magazines from a low shelf. "There's plenty here to keep him busy. It's all out of date, but I don't reckon that matters. It's a good sign if he hasn't forgotten how to read. Maybe some of this will help him remember who he is."

Melissa took the stack of reading material and placed it on the dresser. "I'll take these out to him later." Then she remembered something else. "He asked me for a Bible, but I told him we didn't have one."

Mama used both hands to smooth the wrinkles out of the quilt. "We have one somewhere, Melissa."

"We do? I've never seen it."

Mama circled the bed and dropped to her knees before the old trunk at the foot. When she lifted the lid, a musty odor permeated the room, causing her to cough. "I think it's in here somewhere. It used to belong to my mother." She began to lift things out of the chest and set them one by one on the floor beside her. "Look, Melissa, here's one of your baby dresses. Aw, isn't that sweet?" The tiny batiste garment was yellowed with age. "Oh, and look at this. Here's the dress I got married in. I saved it all these years."

Melissa picked up the soft blue gown and admired the fine pin tucks and hand-embroidered flowers in the bodice. "Who made this for you, Mama?" She held the fragile fabric against her body and twirled around.

"The lady I worked for gave it to me. It was one of hers. I think she felt sorry for me because she knew my own mother was dead, and I didn't have anyone to make a fuss over me." Mama continued to plunge her hands into the trunk and riffle through its contents. At last she found what she was searching for. "Here it is. My mother's Bible. It's the only thing she left me when she died." She handled the black, leather-bound book with reverence.

"Did she read it?" Melissa asked.

"I reckon she did, honey, but I was so little when she died. I don't recollect much about her. Here, you take this out to Dan and tell him he's welcome to read it as much as he wants to."

Melissa held the worn book and turned it over in her hands. "It looks like somebody must have used it a lot. Have you ever read it, Mama?"

Her mother shook her head. "I tried to once, but that was when I was just learning to read, and I didn't get very far. I got bored with all those begats and all, so I just packed it away. I always intended to go back and try again when I got older, but I never got around to it."

Melissa flipped through the pages, scanning a few words here and there, curious as to what caused Dan's interest in it. "I think I'll take it to him now. Maybe he'll tell me what it's all about."

"Don't stay out there too long," Mama cautioned her. "You need to clean those ashes out of the stove so we can make lye soap this week. I packed a few of our bars in Cleve's bag, and we're almost out of it here in the house."

"I won't be long," Melissa promised.

She entered the barn softly lest Dan might be sleeping, but to her surprise, the door to the tack room stood open and Dan was sitting up, his legs sprawled across the hay.

"Look what I brought you," Melissa said, holding up the stack of magazines with Grandmother's Bible resting on top. "This should be enough reading material to last you for a while."

His eyes lit up when he saw the Bible. "So you did have

one after all." He laid the magazines aside, reverently cradling the Bible in his hands.

Melissa was amazed to see him turn through the pages as though his fingers had handled this same book many times before.

"Here it is," he said. "My favorite verse in the whole Bible."

Melissa saw his lips move as he read the words to himself. "What does it say?" she asked. "Read it to me."

" 'For God so loved the world, that he gave his only begotten Son, that whosoever believeth in him should not perish, but have everlasting life.' Isn't that beautiful?"

"I—I guess so. What does it mean?"

"It's talking about Jesus and how God loved us so much that He sent His only Son to earth so that we could live forever and ever. Don't you know about that, Melissa?"

"I've heard people talk about Jesus, but I never had it explained to me like that. What does it mean about everlasting life? It sounds good, but everybody knows we have to die someday."

"Not if you give your heart to Christ, Melissa." For the next hour, Melissa sat spellbound while Dan read and explained verses of scripture to her. Chores were forgotten until she heard her mother's voice shouting from the back steps.

"Melissa, where are you? Are you all right?"

"Yes, Mama. I'm coming," she called. She laid a hand on Dan's arm. "I have to go now, but I want to know more about this. Will you tell me more when I come back?"

Dan's eyes shone with a new light. "It would give me the greatest of pleasure, Melissa." He closed the Bible and stroked its cover tenderly. "There are so many things in this book to share—things that will change your whole life forever."

How could Dan remember so much about Jesus when he didn't even remember his own name? This Jesus must be pretty important to him. Melissa didn't understand all that she had heard today, but even in that brief span of time, she knew with a certainty that Dan possessed something very special—something that she wanted to possess for herself.

❧

Later that same morning, Melissa was hoeing turnips in the garden when she heard the sound of hoofbeats. A few minutes later, her mother called from the back door. "Melissa, come look who's here to see you."

Melissa put down the hoe, leaning it against an oak tree. She supposed Josie Ann had ridden over to discuss her wedding plans. As much as she loved visiting with her friend, she didn't have time today. "Coming, Mama."

Her mother met her on the top step and reached up to straighten her daughter's hair. "Go wash up at the pump first, Melissa. It's that nice Harrison Blake." Mama fidgeted her hands. She was as nervous as a trapped squirrel. "I declare, I wish you had time to change your dress, but there's no time for that now. He's already sitting in the parlor."

Melissa groaned. "Couldn't you just tell him I'm real busy? Ask him to come back later if you must."

"Where are your manners, Daughter? Now you just remember what your father told you, and do as I say."

"Yes, Mama." She might as well get this over with. Melissa trudged across the backyard to the pump to wash the sandy soil from her hands.

eight

When Melissa entered the parlor, Harrison Blake rose to meet her. In his hands, he clutched a bouquet of fragrant, perfectly formed red roses. "These are for you," he said, extending them toward her. "I cut them fresh from my garden this morning." Noting Melissa's reluctance, he added, "I've wrapped the stems to protect your hands from thorns."

Mama stepped forward, smiling broadly. "Here, let me take them. I'll put them in some water." She scurried off, carrying the flowers toward the kitchen. "Melissa just loves roses, don't you, Daughter?"

Melissa thought of her own pitiful little cabbage roses struggling by the front steps. The huge red blooms the tall gentleman handed to her mother looked like they came straight out of the pages of a magazine. She couldn't deny their beauty. "They're lovely. Thank you, Mr. Blake."

"Harrison, please. And may I call you Melissa?"

"Why, yes, of course, Mr. . . .um, Harrison. Won't you sit down? May I fix you a cup of tea?"

Mama returned to the parlor carrying the roses in a pitcher of water. She placed them on a table by the window, positioning a crocheted doily beneath them. Then she retreated to a corner of the room and sat unobtrusively in a slat-backed rocker. With a smile on her lips and her darning basket in her lap, she looked every bit as pleased as a cat that had just captured an elusive mouse.

"Thank you, no." Harrison declined the offer of tea. "I thought, since it's such a lovely spring day, perhaps we might walk in the woods together and become better acquainted."

63

Melissa's face flamed. She didn't have time to walk in the woods, and she had not the slightest desire to become better acquainted with Harrison Blake. She stole a glance at her mother and read the satisfied expectancy in her face. "Thank you, Harrison, but I'm afraid I'll have to decline." This time she avoided looking at her mother, who was sure to be displeased with her reply. "I'm afraid you've caught me at a busy time. I—I have a lot to do today."

"I apologize for not asking ahead of time for permission to call on you, Melissa. Actually, the real reason for my visit was to invite you and your mother to supper at my ranch tomorrow night. I'll send a carriage for you and see that you are safely returned to your home afterward."

Before Melissa could think of an excuse to decline, Mama spoke up. "Why, that's the nicest thing I've ever heard of. Of course we'll come. What time should we be ready?"

"Would four o'clock be too early?" He focused his eyes on Melissa. "That is, if you can finish all those things you have to do by then." Melissa did not miss the sarcasm in his voice.

"Four o'clock will be fine," she said, extending her hand to indicate that the visit was over.

"May I water my horse before I leave? It's rather warm outside, and I'm sure he would appreciate a drink before we start home."

Again, Mama injected herself into the conversation. "Of course you can. Melissa, go with Harrison and show him where to lead his horse around back to the barn. While you're giving him some water, you might as well give him a scoop of grain, too."

"You're too kind, Mrs. Malcolm." He bowed to the lady before he held the front door open for Melissa. "After you, Melissa. I'm sure I could find my way to the barn, but having your company would make the task much more pleasant."

What is Mama thinking? Doesn't she remember that Dan is

in the barn? Has she forgotten we agreed to keep his presence a secret? Melissa gave her mother a meaningful stare before she stepped through the door.

Harrison loosed his horse from the hitching post and followed Melissa through the yard. As they rounded the house, he said, "Since you aren't, um, free to take a little walk in the woods this morning, I'm glad for this chance to speak with you privately, Melissa. I'll have to confess that this request to water my horse was simply an excuse to be alone with you for a few minutes. There are some things I'd like for us to discuss."

The door to the tack room was wide open, and Dan was clearly visible as they approached the barn. She couldn't ignore his presence; she'd have to explain it somehow. "Actually, Harrison, we aren't exactly alone." With a raised palm, she indicated the man seated on the hay. "This is, um, Dan, a friend. Dan, this is Harrison Blake." Hoping to avoid further questions, she pointed toward the watering trough. "Help yourself to the water, Harrison."

Harrison looked momentarily startled, and for a split second, Melissa was sure she saw a spark of recognition in his eyes. Regaining his composure, he nodded to acknowledge the introduction, but neither man spoke. While he attended to his horse's needs, Harrison continued to cast furtive glances at the stranger sitting nearby. Melissa made an unceasing effort to divert his attention with idle chatter. "I declare, Harrison, I do look forward to supper tomorrow night. Mama hasn't been out much since she had the influenza last winter. I'm sure this will be a treat for her." She began walking through the yard and around to the front of the house.

With one long, backward stare at the stranger in the barn, Harrison led his horse and followed. At the front gate, he bade her good-bye before he hurled himself into the saddle. "My carriage will be here for you at four tomorrow," he reminded her. With the spur of his boot, he nudged his horse into a gallop and rode away in a cloud of dust.

❧

After dinner, Melissa put a slab of corn bread on a tin plate and covered it with a generous portion of pinto beans. "This is for Dan," she explained to her mother. "If you want to help me change his dressing, bring a cup of sugar and some of those clean rags I washed yesterday. I'll take a basin of water, and we'll see what that wound looks like today."

They were surprised to see that Dan was standing on his one good leg, balancing himself with the pitchfork. His grin stretched from ear to ear. "See what all your good care has accomplished? If I had a strong, stout stick, I believe I could move around and begin to make myself useful."

Melissa took hold of his right arm and eased him back down on the hay, while her mother stood the pitchfork against the wall.

Melissa placed the basin of water by his side. "It's wonderful to see you getting better, Dan, but I hope you won't give yourself a setback by trying to do too much too soon." She took her seat on the nail keg to begin her work. "I put your dinner in the warming oven to keep hot. I'll bring it to you as soon as we get your dressing changed."

Very gently, she removed the bandages from his shoulder. His forehead was still discolored, but the lump seemed to be slowly receding. *That must have been quite a blow to his head. No wonder he's temporarily lost his memory.* She lifted the poultice from his wound and was gratified to see that the seepage had diminished. She dipped a clean cloth in the basin of water, squeezed it out, and gently bathed his chest.

Dan clinched his eyes and gritted his teeth when she poured fresh sugar into his open wound. Observing his pain, Melissa shuddered, but she couldn't chance allowing him to get an infection. "I'm sorry," she apologized, applying strips of clean cloth to hold the poultice in place. "Just rest for a moment, and I'll go get your dinner."

On their way to the house, Melissa said, "Mama, if Dan can begin to move around a little, isn't it silly for us to keep taking his food all the way out to the barn? Why couldn't he come inside to eat at the table?"

"Honey, don't you remember what we promised your father? I don't want to go against Cleve's wishes."

"Dan could still sleep in the barn, Mama. It would just be for his meals. We wouldn't have to carry food and water back and forth, nor fetch dirty dishes from the tack room. Wouldn't Papa want to make our work easier?" Melissa held her breath while she waited for her mother's answer.

"I don't know, Melissa. I'll have to think about it."

Melissa knew that was as much of an answer as she was going to get for now. She'd just have to wait and hope.

&

Using the overturned nail keg as his table, Dan devoured the pinto beans and corn bread Melissa had brought him. He especially enjoyed the sweet, fresh milk that accompanied every meal. Its familiar taste reinforced his belief that somehow cattle played a part in his background. If only he could remember.

He had spent a pleasant morning perusing the Malcolms' family Bible. Funny that he knew how to find all his favorite passages, yet he couldn't even remember his own name.

In his mind, he kept going over the surprising talk he had shared with Melissa. As far as he knew, he'd never before met anyone who didn't know about Jesus, although he'd encountered many who didn't live by His teachings. How wonderful it had been to introduce Melissa to the Word. She had seemed sincerely interested. Did he dare hope she might make the wonderful decision to become a new person in Christ?

The fellow who came to the barn that morning—Melissa called him Harrison Blake—Dan was sure he had seen him somewhere before. He closed his eyes and tried to remember where they might have met. The man's presence this morning had filled Dan's head with a decidedly unpleasant emotion, though he wasn't sure whether what he felt was fear or hatred. The Bible taught that hate was wrong. Could Harrison Blake pose a threat to him somehow?

Suppose he was never able to remember his past life. He prayed daily for a return of his memory. Surely God would answer his prayers in time, but how long would he have to wait for that answer?

He couldn't stay in this place much longer. As soon as he was able to move around more easily, he'd have to think about leaving. The Malcolms didn't need an extra mouth to feed, especially from someone who couldn't pitch in and help when there was work to be done. It wasn't fair to these people who had been so kind to him.

Where he would go, he had no idea. Maybe if he started out through the woods, his instincts would carry him home. *Home!* The word had a nice ring to it. Did he even have a home? Was anyone looking for him?

He used the last chunk of his corn bread to sop up the juice from the pinto beans, leaving his tin plate so shiny he could see his reflection in it. *Not a pretty sight!* Pieces of his blond hair were still caked with dried blood, and the bump on his forehead made him look deformed.

Laying his soiled utensils aside, he wiped his hands on his britches and picked up the Bible from the hay. He rejoiced to hold the familiar book in his hands. If he continued to read, perhaps something from these pages would help to rekindle his memory.

nine

Admittedly, her own feather mattress was a lot more comfortable for Melissa than the old horsehair settee in the parlor. Nevertheless, worry about Dan deprived her of a peaceful night's sleep. Was he warm enough? Did she hear thunder in the distance? Sometimes the roof of the old barn leaked. And sometimes rats invaded the tack room in search of grain. She shuddered to imagine one of the ugly creatures crawling into Dan's scratchy bed of hay.

Before the rooster crowed, she was dressed and out the back door. "Dan?" she called through the crack in the door. Her heart skipped a beat when she saw the empty stack of hay. "Dan?"

"I'm here, Melissa." Startled, she turned to see him balancing on one leg behind her. "I'm still using this pitchfork for a walking stick, but I was looking around the barn to see if I could find a more suitable prop."

"I'll get something for you," she promised. "I have a couple of hiking sticks I keep to use when I go tramping through the woods. You'd better be careful, though. You don't want to fall and open up that hole in your shoulder. It's just beginning to heal."

She watched him hobble back to the tack room and slump down on the hay. "I feel so useless," he said. "Maybe if you can find me a walking stick, I could start to be of some help around here."

"Healing takes time, Dan. You have to be patient."

Dan repositioned himself on the hay and reached for the Bible. "Would you like to hear what the Good Book has to say about patience?" He smiled as he began to flip through the fragile pages.

Melissa sat down on the upside-down nail keg to listen. "You mean that's in there, too?" To think that this treasured book had lain idle in the bottom of Mama's old trunk for all these years! If only she had known. She had learned to read at her mother's knee when she was only a small child. Why hadn't Mama brought out her Bible then? Melissa could possibly have read the whole thing by now.

Instead of attacking the work waiting for her in the house, she ignored her conscience and settled down on her stool to listen. Dan had the most dramatic, compelling voice she had ever heard. She sat mesmerized by his words. Not until she heard Mama's voice calling from the kitchen door did she jump up from her seat, sending the nail keg flying. "Oh dear! I was so interested in those words, I clean forgot about everything else. I'll come back later, and I'll bring you a stick." She hitched up her skirt and ran.

Mama stood in the doorway. "Melissa, what on earth were you doing out there? You're spending entirely too much time talking to that man. I got tired of waiting for you, so I ate my breakfast alone. I didn't light the fire in the stove because I knew you wanted to collect the ashes. I just crumbled up some of that corn bread and poured buttermilk over it. You'd better come in and eat, too. The sun is already up, and you haven't even milked the cow or gathered the eggs." There was no mistaking the displeasure in her voice.

"I'm sorry, Mama. Dan has been reading to me out of that book you let him use."

"You mean *The Saturday Evening Post*?"

"No, I mean Grandma's Bible. You ought to hear him, Mama. That book is full of wonderful stories, and Dan says they're all true."

Mama scoffed. "I don't want him filling your head up with

nonsense. Religion is for rich people that have time for such. We're just a family of poor farmers, Daughter, and we have to keep our minds on more practical things."

"But Dan says the Bible is for everyone. He says Jesus—"

"Melissa, I don't want to hear any more about what that strange man says. All we need to do is help him get back on his feet so he can leave. Maybe then you'll get your mind out of the clouds and settle down. I declare, Melissa, I've never seen you so addled."

Melissa hadn't realized she had spent so much time in the barn with Dan. She'd have to hurry if she still expected to make a kettle of soap this morning.

"Mama, have you given any more thought to inviting Dan to take his meals inside with us? It would sure make things easier on me, and it would save time, too."

"Oh, I suppose it would be all right. But it's just for meals, mind you. He still sleeps in the tack room."

Melissa tried not to show her delight. Admittedly, she had taken advantage of a situation because she knew how much Mama wanted her to hurry today. She wasn't very hungry, but she buttered a cold biscuit and washed it down with a glass of cold milk.

Hurrying through her breakfast, she took great care to keep the rest of her thoughts to herself.

She shifted her gaze to the cold woodstove. She hated the job of gathering ashes, but it had to be done. Even worse would be the cleanup that followed. Once the ashes were removed, she'd scrub away all the old soot and polish the stove to a clean, black shine. On days like this, she wished for at least one sister—maybe two or three—to spread the work around. She pushed herself away from the table and began her arduous chores.

❧

Noonday sun poured its heat down on the sandy, barren

backyard. Standing over an open fire, Melissa stirred the malodorous mixture in the heavy cast-iron cauldron until her arms ached. She hated the task of soap making, but there was no getting around it; the job must be done.

Earlier, she had leached cold ashes in a barrel from the barn, saving the liquid that oozed from the barrel to mix with rendered lard from the kitchen. Now, as she used her free arm to wipe perspiration from her brow, she wasn't sure which was worse: the cramping muscles in her arm or the horrible stench that assailed her nostrils. She had been stirring the kettle for at least two hours, and still the soap had not solidified.

"Let me give you a hand with that." Melissa hadn't heard Dan come up from behind her.

The walking stick she had given him provided him with a new sense of freedom. He leaned on his makeshift crutch with one hand and stretched out his other to help.

"Dan, you can't stir this pot. You might lose your balance and fall into the fire."

Without answering, he reached across her and wrapped his fingers around the long wooden spoon, gently pulling it from her hand. He did not have to pull very hard, because her muscles were too tired to offer much resistance. "This smells awful," he told her, "but it looks like it's almost ready. Don't you have some mint or chamomile leaves to throw in the pot? Something like that would sure make it smell a heap better."

Melissa looked at him in amazement. How did he know all this? Had he made soap before? Without asking the questions swirling in her brain, she ran to the garden and grabbed a handful of sweet basil stalks. "Will this do?" she asked, returning with her herbs.

"Well, it sure can't hurt. Throw them in the pot, and we'll see."

A welcome breeze lifted the hair from the back of her

neck. "It smells better already, and I think it's boiled long enough. It's beginning to thicken. I'll get a pail of water to douse the fire."

"Melissa?" Mama's shrill call pierced the air.

Melissa reclaimed the wooden spoon. "Go back to the barn, Dan. I'll take care of the fire in a minute. I'd better see what Mama needs."

Mama sounded in a bit of a panic. Melissa ran up the back steps and into the house to see what she needed.

"Melissa, have you forgotten we're going to Harrison Blake's house for supper tonight?"

"Oh, Mama. There's plenty of time. I still have to wash the stove down while it's cold, and I want to finish that dirty job before I wash up and put on clean clothes."

"Daughter, just look at you! Forget the stove until tomorrow. Just get yourself cleaned up, and let's see if we can do something special with your hair."

"Mama, I'll wash up and put on a clean dress, but I don't want to do anything to my hair. I like it fine just the way it is." She flounced out the back door, carrying a pail to the pump.

After filling her pail with water, she doused the flames beneath the soap kettle. It would take a long time for the hot mixture to cool enough to be poured into her pans. She'd have to take care of that later.

She cast a glance toward the barn. Dan certainly seemed to know a lot about making lye soap. He had obviously been involved in the process before. Could this be a clue as to where he came from? Perhaps it indicated he was a married man. That thought had never entered her mind before. She had always pictured a concerned mother and father waiting for their son's return. But a *wife*? Why did that possibility trouble her? Dan could never be anything more to her than a passing stranger she had helped in his time of need, and she'd do well to remember that. She returned to the house with a strangely heavy heart.

A few moments later, she was surprised to hear someone calling her name from the backyard. "Dan?" Sure enough, he stood at the bottom of the steps, using his new walking stick for support.

"I couldn't help but overhear your conversation with your mother, Melissa, and it gave me an idea. Why don't you let me clean that stove for you while you're gone? I can have it spick-and-span before you get back, and it will be ready for a fire in the morning. I can sit on the kitchen floor while I work."

"Oh, Dan, you don't have to do that. You're still recovering from your accident."

"I know I don't *have* to, Melissa, but it would give me a great deal of pleasure to do something to help you and your mother. Can you imagine what it's like to be so completely helpless, to sit back and watch everyone around you working themselves into a frenzy while you do absolutely nothing?"

"Well. . ." Melissa really did dread the stove-cleaning job, but she doubted her mother would allow Dan to stay inside their house while they were away.

But at that precise moment, Mama delivered a surprise. She had heard the entire conversation. "I reckon if Dan wants to clean that old stove, we ought to let him, Melissa. Besides, you don't have time to do it yourself, and you'd never get all that soot cleaned out of your fingernails." To Dan, she said, "I'd be much obliged to accept your offer, Dan. Just mind you, don't make a mess of our nice, clean floor."

Dan smiled. "Yes, ma'am. Don't you worry about a thing, Mrs. Malcolm."

Mama pulled Melissa back into the house and gave her a gentle shove. "Now, get a move on you, girl."

Mama is a surprise a minute!

In the privacy of her room, Melissa slipped out of her

calico skirt and blouse. *My, but today has been a scorcher!* She poured water into her washbowl and began to bathe. The cool water on her sunburned skin felt refreshing. After patting her skin dry with a towel, she dusted her body with cornstarch and pulled a clean gingham frock over her head.

She tried to focus her thoughts on Harrison Blake and the evening ahead, but all she could think about were the amazing words of the blue-eyed stranger taking refuge in her barn. In truth, she no longer thought of him as a stranger at all but rather as a friend. She never dreamed Mama would allow him inside to do a chore. Melissa was sure the concession had been made simply to expedite their preparation for the dinner at the Blake ranch.

She would have preferred to stay at home for supper, especially now that Dan was allowed to eat at their table. She longed to hear him read more of the exciting words from the Bible. He had opened up a whole new world to her with all his talk about Jesus. Was there really a God who cared about her, or was He only for the rich people like Mama said?

She was brushing her hair when her mother rapped on her bedroom door. "Melissa, are you almost ready?" Without waiting for a response, Mama stepped into the room and gave her daughter a critical head-to-toe appraisal. "You're wearing that faded old dress? Why don't you wear the blue one? It's much prettier."

"The blue one has long sleeves," Melissa explained. "I've been out in the sun all day, and I want to be comfortable. Will you braid my hair so I can get it up off my neck?"

Mama sighed. "I wish we had rolled the ends in rags this morning so it would curl a bit for this special occasion. I don't know why you couldn't have been born with a few curls. I declare, I'm so excited about tonight, aren't you?"

Melissa didn't want to dampen her mother's enthusiasm. Mama had experienced little enough excitement in her life lately. "Yes, Mama. I'm sure we'll have a lovely evening." She stood perfectly still while Mama twisted the long strands of her light brown hair into a fancy braid.

ten

Promptly at four o'clock, Melissa heard a knock on the front door. *He's here!* She lingered in her room as long as she dared. If only she could think of some excuse to stay home. Perhaps she should fake an illness and—

"Melissa?" Mama's voice ended her scheming. There was no way out.

"Coming, Mama."

Harrison stood next to her mother in the parlor, his beady eyes appraising Melissa from head to toe. He held a bouquet of roses in his hand. "These are for you, my dear."

Melissa shuddered under his stare. "Thank you, Harrison." She accepted the flowers and turned to find a container for them, but her mother seized them from her hands.

"You stay here in the parlor and talk with Harrison. I'll just put these in some water and be right back."

Alone in the room with Harrison, Melissa bit her lower lip, searching for words to fill the awkward silence. "Um, the roses are beautiful, Harrison." She looked over her shoulder, willing her mother to return.

"Compared to your own beauty, they are but weeds, my dear." He reached for her hand, but she drew back.

"If you'll excuse me for a moment, I think I should fetch my shawl. It might turn cool before we return."

"Actually, it is quite warm this evening. I hardly think you will need a wrap." But Melissa had already hustled out of the parlor, headed for the security of her room.

By the time she returned with her crocheted shawl, Mama stood next to Harrison, scowling at her. There was no mistaking her mother's displeasure, but she was too polite to voice it in front of their guest.

"If you ladies are ready, my carriage awaits," Harrison said.

He held the door open, and Melissa followed her mother toward the gate. *I feel just like that poor little pig must have felt when Papa led him to the slaughterhouse last winter.*

Harrison's Dearborn wagon waited just outside the front gate. His stylish conveyance presented a sharp contrast to the old buckboard in the Malcolms' barn. A young ranch hand with sun-bleached hair sat in the driver's seat.

Harrison assisted the ladies into the wagon before hoisting himself up and claiming a seat between them. "We're all set, Clarence," he called to the driver, and they were on their way.

"My, this is a pleasure," Mama exclaimed. "So much smoother than riding in our old wagon, isn't it, Melissa?"

"What? Oh, yes. Smooth." Melissa's thoughts were occupied elsewhere. "Harrison, your driver looks as though he's been injured. His right shoulder is bandaged, and he appears to have stitches on his arm. What happened to him?"

Harrison shifted his position and hesitated. "He, um, had a little accident awhile back. He isn't able to work cattle right now, so I use him for lighter work like driving my carriage. Say, look at those wild azaleas over there. Aren't they pretty? I love the woods in the springtime."

"Oh, I do, too," Mama agreed. "Melissa does, too, don't you, honey?"

"Um, yes." Melissa's thoughts were churning until she reminded herself that blond-headed ranch hands were a dime a dozen in the Florida Territory and injuries as common as horseflies. There was no reason for her to imagine that this man—

"We're here," Harrison said as the carriage rolled up the circular drive and stopped in front of his long veranda. He jumped down first to assist his guests. "Welcome to my humble abode."

❧

Dan finished the bowl of corn bread and buttermilk that Melissa had slipped out of the house to bring him before she left. She had looked so lovely with her hair braided down her back, although in truth, he liked it best when it hung loose around her shoulders. So many times he had had to restrain his strong impulse to reach out and touch those silky strands.

He finished his meal and set the bowl aside. He'd better get started on that stove. He was sure they would be gone for a long time, but the sun had set, and he was eager to begin.

With the aid of his walking stick, Dan pulled himself up the back steps. Now that he was able to put a little weight on his left ankle, his balance was greatly improved, and movement became easier day by day. Soon a cane would not be needed to help him walk.

He entered the pristine kitchen and eyed the cold woodstove. The thought of helping the Malcolms with a job they deemed unpleasant excited him. Were it not for the kindness of Melissa and her mother, he would likely be dead. He would never be able to repay them, but anything he could do to help them eased his conscience and gave him pleasure.

Someone—probably Melissa—had thoughtfully provided a tub of clean water, a bar of soap, and a pile of rags. He knelt beside the stove, dunked a cloth in water, and began his work.

Though they had left him a candle, he had no need to light it. A full moon sent its golden gleam through the open window and door, bouncing its brilliant rays off the smooth pine floor. How nice to spend an evening indoors away from those eternally whining mosquitoes!

The house was eerily quiet. Outside, he could hear the

same sounds that lulled him to sleep each night—the hoot of a lonely owl, the chirp of crickets, and the chorus of a hundred frogs. Occasionally the grunt of a bull gator pierced the gentle evening medley.

There was a comforting familiarity about these noises. But if he could remember and identify all of these sounds, why couldn't he remember his own name or where he came from? *Dear Lord, will I ever know?* At least he hadn't forgotten how to pray. He counted that his greatest blessing.

And then there was lovely Melissa, certainly a blessing sent from heaven. His feelings for her had spiraled out of control, but he must hide them under the facade of friendship. He had nothing to offer her except a lot of work and worry. Why she tolerated him, he couldn't imagine.

Sometimes his mind played tricks on him. Although he was continually encouraged by fleeting flashes of memory, he found it very frustrating. It was rather like looking through a window but having a curtain drawn just before he could see the very thing for which he was searching. For example, he was certain that somewhere, at some time, he had seen that man who called himself Harrison Blake, but where? The emotion evoked by Blake's presence was not a pleasant one, of that he was certain. But no matter how hard he tried, he just could not remember why.

As he rubbed and scoured the stove, perspiration made little rivers down his sooty face. He was grateful for the cool summer breeze that drifted in from the east. He had been at work for almost an hour when he heard approaching hoofbeats. Were Melissa and her mother coming home from the party already? He needed to get this mess cleaned up before they returned.

Frantically he began to gather the dirty rags into a pile. Carrying everything outside would be a challenge for him, but he was determined to leave the kitchen as clean as he had found it. The cast-iron stove now gleamed in the moonlight like a piece of new coal.

He scooted over to the sawbuck table and used its bench to push himself upright. Old Blue growled from his perch on the top step, a low, menacing snarl. Dan wondered why the lazy hound dog would growl at his own family.

Before he had time to figure that one out, he heard voices, and strangely, they seemed to come from the backyard. He picked up his walking stick and edged toward the door.

The entire area was bathed in silvery moonlight, making it easy for Dan to see the two men on horseback as they approached the barn. He was sure they were up to no good, but what could he possibly do with only a stick for a weapon? He waited and watched.

Old Blue growled again, and Dan noted the raised fur along his brindled backbone. Suddenly, one of the men threw something toward him. Apparently appeased by the gift of a large meaty bone, the hound dog retrieved his treasure and took it to the far corner of the yard.

Voices—even whispers—carry far through open country, especially in quiet night air, and Dan could plainly hear every word the two riders exchanged.

"Where you reckon he be? Boss-man said he'd be in the barn, but there ain't nobody here, as I can see."

"Ain't no tellin'. Maybe he done hightailed it out of here. Whatcha reckon we should do now?"

"I don't know, Shorty, but we can't go back and tell the boss-man we didn't do nothin'. He'd treat us worser than he did that yeller-headed guy we took care of down by Daniel Creek last month."

Dan could feel the hair rising on the back of his neck. He inched closer to hear more.

"Ain't no need to shoot until we find him. How 'bout we set fire to the barn? Thataway, if he be hidin' in there, he'll be burned to a crisp. If he took off, we won't have to worry 'bout him nohow."

The man called Shorty cackled a wicked laugh. "Let's do it!"

Dan stood at the door feeling as helpless as a treed squirrel. Bitter bile rose in his throat. He must find some way to stop their sinister plot, but how? These men were armed and dangerous. And just who was this boss-man they kept referring to?

He caught a glimpse of a quick flicker of flame before he heard a shout. "Let's get out of here quick."

The two criminals galloped away so fast that Dan didn't fear them noticing him as he dashed from the house and hobbled across the yard with a tub of dirty water in his hands.

Excruciating pain shot up his leg as his feet bore the full weight of his body. The tub of water added even more weight to his load, but he couldn't afford to worry about that now. He had to act fast, no matter what the cost to his body. He slung water on the growing flame and ran to the pump for more. Thankfully, he was able to douse the flame before it reached the hay. A fire in the haystack would have ignited the whole barn in minutes, and the house would have soon followed. Dan made several trips back and forth between the pump and the barn, until he was sure that every ember was extinguished. Only then did he hobble into the house to wipe the last traces of soot and grime from around the stove with a clean rag and dispose of the debris from his night's work.

At last he returned to the barn and collapsed on his bed of straw, too exhausted to worry about the pain shooting from his ankle all the way up his calf. Besides, he had more pressing matters to worry about than physical pain. What did all this mean? Who were those men, and who had sent them on such an evil mission? His only clues lay in the words he had overheard and a fleeting glimpse of a brand on one of their horses. Was his mind playing tricks on him again, or did he plainly see a horse's rump seared with the letter B?

What should he do next? Should he warn Melissa and her mother of the dangerous outlaws who had almost destroyed their little homestead tonight? The Malcolms could easily have lost everything they owned to those hungry flames, and all because of the vicious act of two evil men.

The part that puzzled him most was the words he had overheard. It seemed that the Malcolm family was not the real target of their mischief. No, these scoundrels were out to get *him*. But why? What terrible thing had he done to make someone hate him so much? If only he could remember. And unless his ears deceived him, this whole ugly plot had been devised by someone these men referred to as their boss.

The pungent smell of smoke lingered in the air, a bitter reminder of what had happened. Of one thing he was certain: This vengeance would not end here. His enemies would return, just as sure as the sun returned each morning. And Dan was certain they would stop at nothing until they killed him.

The terrible truth hit him with the force of a fist planted in the pit of his belly. His presence here was putting Melissa and her mother in serious jeopardy. There was only one thing to do. He couldn't stay here and be a source of trouble for them. He must leave them at once and strike out on his own.

&

Mama's eyes devoured every amenity on the beautifully appointed table, from the fine embroidered linen cloth to the gleaming silver and crystal sparkling in the light of a dozen candles. Melissa read the hope in her eyes and knew exactly what Mama had on her mind.

Thankfully, Melissa had no need to concern herself with maintaining a flow of conversation. Leaving no awkward gaps of silence, her mother paused between each delicious bite to voice her pleasure at her surroundings.

"I declare, Harrison, this roast pork fairly melts in my

mouth. I must ask your cook to show me how she manages to get it so tender."

"I'm glad you're enjoying it, Mrs. Malcolm. And how about you, Melissa? May I offer you a biscuit?"

"No, thank you. I—"

"Melissa makes biscuits that are light as a feather," Mama interjected. "My daughter is a wonderful cook. You should taste one of her sweet potato pies."

"Mama, *please*. . ."

Harrison hid his smile behind his napkin. "I hope to have that pleasure one day soon."

"And you shall," Mama promised. "We'd be pleased to have you drop in for supper anytime, wouldn't we, Melissa?" Without waiting for Melissa's answer and without acknowledging the telling glare in her daughter's eyes, she blustered on. "How about next Saturday?"

Melissa almost choked on her water. Pressing her napkin to her lips, she took a moment to recapture her composure, while Mama's question hung in the air like an ominous insect waiting to sting.

"Um, I'm afraid we can't plan on next Saturday. I, um, I think I may need to make a trip to Milltown on Saturday," Melissa spluttered.

"Milltown? Whatever for? Don't you remember? You just went there last week and stocked up on supplies. You won't need to go again until next month."

"Yes, I know, Mama, but I told Josie Ann I'd come back soon to help with her wedding plans, and I, um, need to go back to the commissary to, um, to pick out some fabric for that new dress Papa promised me."

Harrison's low voice at the end of the table startled her. "Melissa, I'd consider it a privilege if you would allow me to drive you to Milltown in my carriage. You might find it to be a smoother ride, and it would give me an opportunity to discuss with you something I—"

"How nice!" Mama clapped her hands in delight. "Melissa complained about riding over that rough trail in our old buckboard. I declare, that's the nicest thing I ever heard of, isn't it, Melissa?"

Melissa could feel the blood rushing to her cheeks. "Yes—I mean, *no!*" Embarrassed by her spontaneous outburst, she lowered her tone an octave and explained. "That is very kind of you, Harrison, but I just couldn't permit you to do it. You see, I don't know how long I might stay at Josie Ann's—maybe even overnight. Anyway, I'm quite accustomed to riding in our wagon, so I really don't mind the drive at all."

The Spanish maid had cleared the table as they talked and now began to serve dessert. She placed a stemmed crystal dish of pudding at each place, along with a tiny cup of strong, aromatic coffee.

"Egg custard?" Melissa asked, eager to turn the conversation in a different direction. "That's one of my favorites."

"Flan," Harrison explained, "is a delicate Spanish custard with a rich caramel sauce on the bottom. I like it very much, so Isabella makes it often. I hope you enjoy it, too." He picked up his spoon and made no more mention of the invitation to supper or to the trip to Milltown. For the first time that evening, the room became quiet except for the gentle clink of spoons against crystal as the three diners finished their meal in silence.

eleven

The ride home proved strained and uncomfortable. Mama was as mad as a cat in a washtub, and she made little effort to conceal her feelings. Melissa thought that if the circumstances were not so serious, she would find Mama's behavior comical. Her polite remarks to Harrison were interspersed with short, cryptic sentences addressed to Melissa. Harrison's talk was limited to mundane observations about the weather. When at last their modest little home came into sight, Melissa heaved a sigh of relief.

The driver stopped in front of the gate and waited while Harrison hopped out and assisted the ladies to the ground. "Just hold it there for a minute, Clarence. I'll be right back."

Harrison saw them to the door and bade them good night. "Thank you for a lovely evening," Melissa said before she stepped into the dark sanctuary of the parlor.

Mama lingered on the porch, telling Harrison over and over again how much she had enjoyed herself. Melissa thought she overdid her enthusiasm. But she wasn't prepared for what she heard next, coming out of the mouth of her very own mother.

"Harrison, I do hope you'll forgive my daughter's behavior tonight. I fear she didn't feel well."

Melissa had a strong urge to shout through the door that she felt very well, thank you very much, but instead, she stood quietly listening.

"No apology is necessary, Mrs. Malcolm. I hope none of my food disagreed with her. Perhaps she'll feel better by tomorrow."

"I'm sure she will," Mama declared. "She's not a delicate girl, Harrison. She's really very healthy, and—"

"Yes, well, give her my best regards."

Melissa heard his footsteps crunch across the yard. She clutched her head with both hands and sank to the floor in humiliation.

Mama was barely inside the door before she began scolding her daughter. "Melissa, I hope you're satisfied with yourself. You just may have thrown away your only chance to live like a princess for the rest of your life. Rich bachelors don't come along every day, especially out here in the wilderness. What on earth got into you, Daughter?" She crossed the room and lit a candle.

Melissa pushed herself up from the floor. "I'm tired, Mama. Can't we talk about this tomorrow?" She lit another candle and carried it toward the kitchen.

"Very well, Melissa. If you want to live the rest of your life like a poor dirt farmer, that will be your choice. I fear you've been spending too much time reading love stories in those magazines Josie Ann gives you. But you might take a moment to consider how you could help your hardworking parents who've struggled day after day, year after year, to achieve a better lifestyle for us all."

"Mama, come look at this!"

Her tirade momentarily forgotten, Mama carried her candle into the kitchen, where Melissa stood gaping at the old woodstove, its ebony surface gleaming in the candlelight.

"Well, I never!" Mama ran her fingers over the cold cast iron. "Why, it looks plumb new," she exclaimed. "I don't know how he did it."

"And not a spot of soot on the floor. It's a miracle," Melissa agreed. "I'm going to the barn to thank him before I go to bed." She blew out her candle and hurried out the back door before her mother had a chance to protest.

She lifted her skirts and ran across the ground. What was that strange smell? The acrid aroma of smoke hung in the air like a hovering cloud. "Dan?" The tack-room door stood ajar, and she could see him sitting on the nail keg beside his bed of hay, his head cradled in his hands.

"I thought you might be asleep," she said, "but I wanted to thank you for cleaning our cookstove. It hasn't looked like that since the day Papa bought it at the commissary. I'm going to hate messing it up with a fire tomorrow morning."

"I'm glad I could do something for you, Melissa. You've been so good to me."

His voice sounded odd, strained somehow, as though he carried a great sorrow. Then she saw his outstretched leg and gasped. His britches were rolled up, and his left ankle bulged to almost double its normal size. "Oh, Dan, I shouldn't have let you do it. Just look at your ankle. It's as bad as when I first brought you home, and it's all my fault." She dropped to her knees and examined it in the moonlight.

"It's not your fault, Melissa. I confess I strained it tonight, but it had nothing to do with my work in the house. You see, there was a—a little accident—a fire in the corner of the barn, but I managed to douse it before it got started, and I'm afraid I aggravated my ankle in the process."

"A fire? How could that be?" She glanced at the cloudless, moonlit sky. "There was no lightning tonight."

"Don't worry about it now. It's over, and there's no damage done." Dan raised his head and focused his eyes on her face. "My, but you look lovely tonight."

Her heart soared at his compliment. "Thank you." Flustered, she motioned toward his little mound of hay. "Lie down on your bed," she commanded. "I'm not happy about your injury. I'm going to prop your foot up on a stool. I'll come out and look at it again in the morning, but you must promise me you'll keep it elevated all night. We need to get that swelling down."

She saw him grimace as he slid over on the hay, but in spite of his pain, he smiled at her. "Yes, ma'am."

She fetched her milking stool from the barn and padded it with a saddle blanket. Lifting his foot as gently as possible, she placed it on the stool. "There now." She covered him with his quilt, pulling it up to his chin. Her hand trembled as her fingers brushed against his chin. "Try to sleep. We'll talk again tomorrow."

By the time she returned to the house, her mother had already gone to bed. At least she wouldn't have to listen to more of Mama's criticism of her behavior tonight. Knowing the importance her mother had placed on creating a favorable impression, Melissa had minded her table manners and she had thanked Harrison for the outing. Should she pretend to care for Harrison Blake, when in truth, his presence frightened and upset her? Wouldn't that be like telling a lie? Mama had always taught her that lying was wrong. And she couldn't imagine marrying and spending her life with that man, no matter how wealthy he might be. If she couldn't find a man whom she loved and respected, then she'd rather never marry at all.

Her thoughts turned to Dan. Now, there was a man she could learn to love. In fact—but no, she mustn't allow her mind to go in that direction. He probably had a wife already, maybe even a child, watching and waiting for his return. She must go back to Milltown at once to see what new information she could discover.

As much as it pained her to think about Dan's departure, she must help him return to his own home as soon as possible. Every day he stayed in her barn just made it that much harder to think of losing him.

There was no way on earth this mystifying man could ever play a part in her future. But no matter how much she tried to deny it, she knew that he had already captured her heart.

❧

Dan placed both hands beneath his head and tried to decide what to do. He had thought to strike out before daybreak tomorrow, freeing Melissa and her mother of the danger of his presence, but the throbbing pain in his ankle erased the idea of walking anywhere. Even with the aid of a stick, he couldn't hope to walk far. Not until he healed. How long would healing take? Even more importantly, how long before his predators returned?

He tried to think what he could have done differently that would have prevented further injury to his leg. But under the same circumstances, he knew he would do the same thing over again, no matter what the personal cost. He'd have no choice. If he had been able to confront the men before they set the fire, could he have stopped them? Two armed men? Never.

If he could just remember his past, to know what reason someone might have for wanting him dead, perhaps then he could make amends and put the matter to rest.

So many "ifs." *But you can't dam up flowing water.* Something he had done in the past must have precipitated tonight's events.

Until he could remember his home and his family, or even if he had one, he would feel completely alone in this world. No, that was wrong. He had at least one friend he could always count on, a friend who was willing to share all his burdens and sorrows. *Lord, am I a thief or a murderer? I don't know what terrible thing I have done to warrant this hatred, but whatever it is, please forgive me.*

❧

Before the dew was dry on the ground, Melissa was out the back door and across the yard. "Dan?" she called softly, in case he might still be asleep.

"Good morning, Melissa."

At the sound of his voice, she pushed open the tack-room door. He lay on the hay, just as she had left him, his left leg elevated on the milk stool. A quick glance told her he was much better. "Did you sleep well in spite of your pain?"

"Like a bear in winter," he assured her. "Look, your plan worked. The swelling has gone down. I think, if you give me my walking stick, I could move around a bit." He slid his leg off its prop and returned her milking stool. "You'll be needing this soon. I've already heard Flossie calling you."

Melissa put the stool on the ground and sat on it. "Flossie can wait," she said with a grin. "I'm fixing to make a pot of grits as soon as the stove heats up, and I'm going to make some biscuits, too. I sure hated to start a fire in that nice, clean stove this morning, but I figured we could all do with a good breakfast. And guess what? Mama says it'll be all right for you to eat at the table with us from now on. That is, if you think you can get up those steps."

"Nothing could stop me," he said. "I've tasted your biscuits before, and I'd swim a river if I had to."

Melissa laughed. "That won't be necessary." She handed him his walking stick. "Take your time. Breakfast won't be ready for a while. Just come whenever you're ready. Holler, and I'll help you up the steps." She took a step toward the door.

"I think I'll be able to manage by myself, thank you. I'll come to the house right after I finish my morning devotions." He reached for the Bible. "Last night when I prayed, I asked Jesus to help heal my ankle, and just look at it this morning. I need to thank Him for that."

Melissa turned around and stared at him. "Dan—" She stopped her sentence abruptly.

"What is it, Melissa?" he prompted. "What did you want to say?"

"Well, I just wanted to ask you. . . . Dan, could you teach me to pray?"

"Come back and sit down, Melissa. Surely it won't matter if we hold up breakfast for a few minutes. I want you to sit here beside me. We're going to pray together."

Melissa replaced the stool beside the hay, and Dan reached for her hands. "Melissa, would you like to invite Jesus into your heart today so that you can live forever in a place He has prepared for you?"

Tears stung the back of her eyes. "I'd like that very much, but I'm not sure He has time for the likes of me. I'm just an ordinary country girl. Mama says—"

Dan squeezed her fingertips, and something inside her seemed to explode, opening her eyes to a whole new vision—a vision in which she, Melissa Malcolm, could be part of God's family forever. Was such a thing possible?

"I mean no disrespect to your mother, Melissa, but you can be as sure as the sunrise at dawn that God loves you, and He wants you for one of His own."

With her eyes closed, Melissa repeated the words Dan taught her, thanking Jesus for His tremendous sacrifice. When she asked Him to wash away her sins and give her a new beginning, she knew her life would never be the same again.

twelve

Dan sat across the table from Melissa and her mother, enjoying his breakfast of grits and eggs. "Thank you for inviting me to your table, Mrs. Malcolm. This is food fit for a king." He helped himself to a biscuit from the blue enameled plate and slathered it with fresh butter and guava jam.

"It's the least I could do after the way you polished up our stove last night." Mama lifted a cup of coffee to her lips. "I reckon we'll have orange juice with our breakfast tomorrow. That nice Harrison Blake promised to bring us a bag of fruit from his trees today." She nudged Melissa. "Honey, would you like for me to roll your hair in rags this morning so it'll curl up pretty before he gets here?"

Melissa squirmed on the hard wooden bench. "No, thank you, Mama. It's just fine the way it is." She filled her mouth with coffee, hoping to end the discussion before it escalated beyond her control. She had more important things on her mind this morning. She had soared to a mountaintop, and she wasn't ready to come down.

Mama gave her a sidewise glance. "Dan, I reckon you've noticed there's a new sparkle in my daughter's eyes this morning."

Dan winked at Melissa. "Yes, ma'am, I noticed she did look mighty happy today." The smile never left his face, even as he drank his coffee.

"Well, can you guess why she's so happy?" A smug, self-satisfied expression spread over Mama's face.

Dan raised his eyebrows to question Melissa, but Melissa shook her head and raised her finger to her lips. "Why don't you tell me, Mrs. Malcolm?"

"Well, I don't want to let the cat out of the bag ahead of time. Let's wait until Papa returns and Harrison has a chance to talk to him." She turned her attention to the food on her plate, maintaining her secretive demeanor. "I reckon Melissa will tell us when she's ready."

Why did Mama persist in thinking Melissa would consider a serious relationship with Harrison Blake? She had told her over and over again that she had no intention of ever letting that happen. "I have every reason to be happy this morning," Melissa declared, "and despite what you think, it has nothing to do with Harrison Blake." She picked up her cup and plate and rose from the table. "You two take your time. I'm going to start my chores. I have a lot of work to do if I'm to go to Milltown on Saturday."

"Daughter, there's no need—"

But Melissa left the room before her mother could protest. Nothing could mar her happiness on this wonderful day, not even the impending visit from her neighbor to the north. She was a new person in Christ, and He had a plan for her life! She didn't yet know what that plan entailed, but she was quite sure it did not include Harrison Blake.

She hummed as she vigorously wielded her pine needle broom. She had a few plans of her own, which she intended to discuss with Mama while she remained in such a good mood.

Halfway through the morning, she heard the approach of a horse. She busied herself at the farthest corner of the house, hoping that Mama would accept Harrison's gift of oranges and send him on his way. But, of course, she knew that was never going to happen.

"Melissa, come see who's here."

She wrung out her rag mop into the pail and stood it against the wall. There was no escape. How long would it take Harrison to realize she had no interest in his courtship?

She heard her mother call again, impatiently this time. "Just a minute, Mama. I'm coming."

Their voices carried from the next room as Mama tried to explain her daughter's absence. "She's in there prettying up a bit before she sees you, Harrison. You know how these young girls are. My, what big, juicy oranges. Just set them on the kitchen table for me, and I'll squeeze them after a bit."

Melissa entered the room just as Harrison returned from the kitchen. Long, errant strands of brown hair escaped from the gingham scarf she wore to protect her head from dust while cleaning. Perspiration beaded on her forehead. She swiped her hands on her apron and extended a cool, cordial greeting to her visitor. "Good morning, Harrison. It is very kind of you to share your fruit with us." The firm grip of his hand sent an unpleasant shiver up her spine. She drew back and stood close to the front door, hoping he would take the hint and leave.

"Can't you sit a spell?" Mama invited. "I'll fetch you a glass of cold spring water while you and Melissa sit here and talk." Without waiting for his answer, she moved toward the kitchen, leaving the two of them alone in the parlor.

Melissa had little choice but to sink down on the stiff horsehair upholstery. She positioned herself in the center of the settee and spread her skirts as wide as possible to dispel any notion he might have of sitting next to her. "Please have a seat." She motioned to a simple, slat-backed chair, and Harrison eased his frame onto its narrow-caned bottom.

"I'm very glad for a few minutes to visit with you." He leaned forward and tried to capture her attention. "We seem to have little opportunity to talk alone." He looked over his shoulder to satisfy himself that no other ears overheard his words. "I have some exciting plans ahead for myself and my ranch, and I hope you will consider being a part of those plans, my dear."

Melissa's cheeks burned, but while she struggled to think of a suitable reply, the back door slammed and Mama reentered the parlor carrying a frosted jar of cold water. Melissa had never been happier to see anyone in her life. She pushed over to the side of the settee and gathered in her skirts. "Sit here by me, Mama."

Harrison was too polite to show his displeasure. Instead, he smiled. "Indeed, Mrs. Malcolm. Do sit with us. Actually, I have a matter I want to discuss with the both of you."

Melissa cringed. She had been sure he would wait for Papa's return to formally ask for her hand in marriage. But Harrison's next words, totally unrelated to marriage, surprised her.

"It's about that, er, visitor you have out back in your barn. Has he left yet?"

"No, he's still here."

Why is he interested in a man he doesn't even know? "We don't like to turn people away from our door when they're in need," Melissa explained. "He's been injured, and he isn't able to travel yet, but he's improving. He'll likely be on his way before long. Why do you ask?"

"No reason," Harrison responded quickly—too quickly, Melissa thought. "I just feel a strong responsibility to you and your mother while your father is away, and I'm afraid this stranger's presence might present a real danger. You said he doesn't remember anything about his, um, accident or any events from his past?"

"Not yet, but his memory is returning by bits and pieces. I think it only a matter of time before he recalls what happened to him."

Harrison shifted his weight, and the little chair creaked beneath him. "Mrs. Malcolm, I believe you should insist that he leave at once. Why, you and Melissa could be murdered in the middle of the night. There are many evil men lurking in the Florida Territory. You know nothing about this man's background. I hope you'll take my advice and send him on his way this very day."

Melissa glared at him. "Mr. Blake, it plainly states in the Bible that we are to feed the hungry and give shelter to the homeless." She felt her mother's eyes on her. "We are merely extending kindness to a man in need."

Harrison was obviously taken aback. "Of course. Well, that is very generous of you, and I'm sure he appreciates it. But I strongly believe there should be a limit to your generosity, especially when safety is a concern." Balancing his arms on his thighs, he leaned forward. "Now, I want to help you two lovely women, so I have devised a plan. I can put that man on my horse and give him a ride out into the countryside. I will probably be doing him a big favor. Perhaps he might see something out there to trigger his memory. In any case, I will make certain that he doesn't trouble you further."

Melissa paled. She stood, hoping to precipitate an end to the visit. "That will not be necessary, Harrison. Our visitor has been no trouble. We're just very happy we could help him." She straightened her skirts and pushed straggling strands of hair back from her face. Her tone was cool and distant. "Thank you so much for your concern for our safety. We'll take your words into consideration. And now, if you'll excuse me, I have many things I must do today. . . ."

Harrison rose from his chair, but an obviously distressed Mama was immediately on her feet in front of him. "You don't have to go yet, Harrison. I'll do some of Melissa's chores so she can visit with you a little longer." She gave her daughter a meaningful glare. "Harrison has come all this way to see you, Melissa. Surely your work can wait for a minute or two."

Harrison looked at Melissa for confirmation, and finding none, he stepped toward the door. "I'm afraid I also have things to do today, so I'll be on my way. But please, think about what

I've said, Mrs. Malcolm. That man has a dangerous look about him, and I don't think it's wise to keep him around. If you change your mind and want me to help, just let me know. I'll be checking back with you from time to time."

Melissa returned to her bedroom where her rag mop and pail awaited her, leaving her mother to see Harrison out the door. She would be in for a scolding, no doubt, but she simply couldn't tolerate another minute in the same room with that horrible man. Just thinking of his touch made her flesh crawl.

thirteen

As the days rolled by, robins began to sing from the oak trees and build their nests among the branches, and the barren earth began to sprout sprigs of new growth, sure signs that summer was just around the corner.

"When I go to the commissary tomorrow, I'll purchase seed for our garden," Melissa announced across the breakfast table. "I'd like to get our vegetables in the ground before the summer showers begin."

Mama poured a thin stream of molasses over the stack of hoecakes on her plate. "Be sure you put in plenty of tomato plants this time. I want to make sure we have enough jars next winter. We've already used all the ones I put up last year."

"Yes, and the pole beans, too. If this pretty weather holds up, I can start staking out the rows next week."

Dan lowered his coffee cup from his lips and set it on the table. "I'd like to help with that garden, if you'll allow me."

Mama's pleasure radiated from her face. "That would be wonderful if you could. I worry that Melissa has so much work to do, and there's no telling when Cleve will be home to help."

Melissa looked skeptical. "Are you sure you're up to it, Dan? Remember what happened to your ankle when you cleaned the stove. You mustn't overdo. We don't want any more setbacks."

"I'd truly enjoy it," he assured them. "I know I've done it before. I remember planting seeds in straight rows and then the joy of watching the tender green plants emerge. I used to put up string between stakes to make sure I got the rows lined up perfectly straight."

"Oh, Dan, just listen to you! You're remembering more and more every day. It's only a matter of time before you recall everything from your past." Melissa's heart filled with a surge of bittersweet joy. Of course she wanted Dan to recover completely. In fact, now that he had taught her how to talk to God, she prayed daily for his return to health. But when that day finally arrived, she knew that Dan would leave them and be gone from her forever. How would she ever be able to endure life without him?

Melissa squeezed her eyes tightly shut to hold back her tears because she knew if the first one fell, there would be no stopping the deluge that would follow. She swung her legs over the oak bench and stood, turning her back to them. "Well, I can't sit here all day. You people can sit here and drink coffee if you want to, but I have a wash to get on the line." She pulled a handkerchief from her apron pocket and dabbed at her eyes as she left the room to gather up her laundry.

❧

Two hours later, Melissa lugged her basket of wet clothes to the backyard line. She wore a wide-brimmed calico bonnet to protect her face from the searing Florida sunlight. She had just hung the first sheet on the line when Dan approached, hobbling along without his walking stick.

"See how I'm walking on my own?" he boasted. He bent to pick up another sheet and fastened it to the clothesline.

"You don't have to do this, Dan. Washday is women's work."

"Who made that rule? Besides, I've done this before." He continued to work beside her until the lines were full and her basket empty. "There now. Someone used to tell me 'many hands make light work.' That someone must have been my mother."

"I've heard that saying, too. It's true, isn't it? Look how quickly we got the job done." She picked up her basket and propped it against one hip. "Thank you for helping me."

Dan made no move to walk away. "I was just wondering about something. I saw a hoe in the barn. If you show me where you want your garden, I could start loosening up the soil to get it ready for the seeds."

"I reckon we'll put it right back there where we've always had it," she said, waving her free hand to indicate the east corner. A few broken stakes jutted from the ground and stood at irregular angles, holding the withering remains of a previous harvest. "There's not much left there now." She shook her head. "I don't know, Dan. I'm not sure you're ready to take on a job like that yet."

"Let me be the judge of that," he pleaded. Melissa thought he looked like a small boy begging for a piece of candy. "I'll only do a little at a time, I promise. I just want to get started doing something to make myself useful around here."

Before she could answer, their attention was diverted. A horse whinnied in the distance, accompanied by the sound of approaching hoofbeats. *Oh no! Not him again!*

"I think I'll go to the springhouse and check on what supplies we might need from the commissary."

Dan hobbled back to the barn as Melissa set her basket on the steps and hurried across the backyard. The springhouse was out of sight and as far away as she could hope to get. Maybe, just maybe, her mother would leave her be.

Moments later, her hopes vanished when she heard Mama's shrill call. "Melissa? Where are you? There's someone here to see you."

"I'm out back, Mama," she yelled, making no effort to halt her work. Only when she heard the back door slam did she admit defeat. She didn't want Harrison to corner her here in the springhouse. Instead, she walked halfway across the yard to meet him in the open. "Good morning, Harrison."

"Good morning, Melissa." He pulled a fine linen hand-kerchief from his pocket and swiped it across his brow. He deliberately held it so that his monogram showed. "Could we go inside to get out of the sun? Your mother suggested we might have a glass of cool orange juice."

Melissa shifted her gaze between the back door and the springhouse, trying to decide on the lesser of two entrapments. "Did you have something specific you wanted to say? Because I'm in the midst of cleaning out our cooler, and I'd like to finish before noon."

Harrison transferred his weight from one leg to the other, letting his face reveal his displeasure. He was a man accustomed to having things his own way. "I have several things I came to talk about, but I hardly think this is the place to discuss them."

"Then perhaps another time would be better." Melissa stood her ground in the middle of the sandy yard.

From the corner of her eye, she saw Dan emerge from the barn carrying a hoe. He moved with surprising speed, considering his strange gait, and headed for the garden plot in the east corner.

Harrison glared at him. "There goes one of my reasons for coming. I see that stranger is still hanging around. He's even carrying a hoe. Melissa, something as simple as that hoe could become a lethal weapon if he should decide to use it as such. I must insist that you let me take him away from here. I'll make sure you've seen the last of him."

Even under the scorching sun, a chill coursed through Melissa's body. Harrison's words posed an ominous threat to Dan's welfare—yes, even to his very life—and Melissa was the only one who could protect him. "Harrison, you need to understand something. We no longer consider Dan as a stranger. To us, he has become a friend. I want you to forget any thoughts you may have about taking him away. He is a grown man, and we will let him decide for himself when he chooses to leave. When that time comes, he will make his own decision on where and how he will travel. Now, if you'll excuse me, I need to finish my chores."

Harrison's face reddened with rage. "This kind of irresponsible thinking points out just how immature you really are, Melissa. Your father has good cause to be worried about you."

The tension between them simmered like a teapot ready to burst its lid and explode. "My father has a great deal more compassion than you do, Harrison. He has given his permission for Dan to take shelter in our barn."

"Dan? How do you know his name?"

"It's not his real name. It's just one I gave him so we don't have to keep calling him 'the stranger.' We'll know his real name soon, though. His memory is returning by leaps and bounds."

Harrison looked as startled as though he had received a splash of cold water in his face. His raging flush was replaced by a sudden pallor. "What lies has that scalawag told you?"

She looked at him with eyes as cold as a winter storm. "He has told us no lies."

Harrison jerked his body around and headed for the house, shouting all the way. "I'm going inside to talk to your mother. I am sure she has more common sense and much better judgment than you. It would behoove you, young lady, to pay closer attention to her advice."

Melissa turned to see Dan watching from the corner of the barn. She gave a fleeting look at Harrison's back before she hurried across the yard toward Dan.

His ashen face told Melissa that he had heard every word. He leaned against the hoe. "Melissa, I have to get away from here. That man is part of my past. Even though I can't remember just where he fits in, I know he represents a real threat to my life. I can't continue to put you and your mother in such a dangerous position." He straightened and gripped the handle of the hoe with his right hand. "I promised to help ready your garden, but as soon as I'm finished with that, I've made up my mind to leave."

Melissa felt her whole world crumbling beneath her feet. She had always known that he would leave someday, but she had imagined when that time came, he would return to some safe haven that awaited him. To strike out now without a clue to his destination—Where would he go? How would he exist? Without a miracle, the situation was beyond hope. Was there no one who understood?

"For I know the thoughts that I think toward you, saith the Lord, thoughts of peace, and not of evil, to give you an expected end. Then shall ye call upon me, and ye shall go and pray unto me, and I will hearken unto you." Melissa had memorized those words when Dan first read them to her from her grandmother's Bible, and now they came rolling into her mind like a tidal wave. She took a deep breath and looked into Dan's startling blue eyes. "Don't make any decision about leaving yet. Let's both pray about it."

&

By the time the sun reached midway in the sky, Melissa called out the back door. "Dan, dinner is ready."

Mama had prepared a pot of her special recipe for chicken and dumplings. Melissa drained her boiled cabbage salad and piled it into a bowl. She lifted a pan of corn bread from the warming oven and set it on the table.

After washing his hands at the pump, Dan came in through the kitchen door. "It sure smells good in here." He took his place at the table and bowed his head.

"Why do you always do that before you eat?" Mama asked when he raised his head.

"I'm just taking a minute to thank God for my many

blessings," Dan said. "It's something I've done all my life."

"I'd like to do that, too," Melissa said. "Could you teach us how, Dan?"

Dan looked to Mama for permission. Noting her nod, he bowed his head once more, and the two women did likewise. "Dear Father, we thank You for the bounteous goodness Your hands have provided for this table. Help us use this nourishment to the service of Your kingdom. In Jesus' name we pray. Amen."

Melissa raised her head and studied her mother's face. Encouraged by Mama's pleased and peaceful reaction to the prayer, she decided the time was right to approach her mother again on a subject dear to her heart. "Mama, Dan has been teaching me things from the Bible. I've asked Jesus to come into my heart and give me a new beginning. It's a wonderful feeling, Mama. It means I'll live with Him forever. Wouldn't you like to hear about it, too?" She held her breath while she watched Mama wrestle with a soul-wrenching decision.

Mama took a long time to answer. "I don't remember much about my mother, but I do know she lived by the words in the Bible. But I've lived without it for so long, I reckon Jesus has given up on me by now. No, Daughter, I'm happy if you've found a better way of life, but I'm afraid it's too late for me."

"I mean no disrespect, Mrs. Malcolm, but you're wrong. Won't you please let me show you what it says about that in the Bible?"

Melissa waited silently while her mother ruminated on the idea. "I reckon it wouldn't do any harm to listen," she finally acquiesced. "Let's eat our dinner now before it gets cold. After we get done, we can sit here at the table, and you can tell me about it; but mind you, I'm not promising anything."

Melissa's heart swelled with joy. God had opened a door

that could be the answer to one of her deepest prayers. Once Mama learned of God's wonderful promises to the world and how He sacrificed His only Son to give eternal life to all who believed in Him, she would surely reach out and give her life to Jesus. Then Mama would be a part of His glorious kingdom, just as she and Dan were. She picked up her fork and began to eat. Chicken and dumplings had never tasted so good!

fourteen

Early Saturday morning, Melissa readied the family wagon for the long ride to the commissary. She had planned to leave at daybreak, but she couldn't leave all the chores for her mother. Mama seemed stronger each day, but she was still a long way from full recovery.

"Get a move on, Daughter. I thought you'd be halfway there by this time." Mama fixed her eyes on the kitchen window. "The sun is up already."

"I'm almost ready, Mama. I put a jar of your pickled eggs in my basket. Mr. Whittamore is always happy to get those for barter. Are you sure you've written down everything you'll need?"

"Yes, I'm sure. Here now. Here's the money Papa left, with extra for our dresses. Pick out a pretty muslin print for me, and get something bright and colorful for yourself. Maybe you'll find some ribbon for trim."

"I've been thinking, Mama. My blue dress will do just fine for Josie Ann's wedding. I don't really need anything new. Dan has worn those same clothes ever since he's been here. They're not going to hold up through many more washings. I thought I might get some denim for a new pair of britches and enough gingham for a shirt. Would you help me with the sewing?"

Mama frowned. "Your blue dress has long sleeves. It'll be much too hot. You need something new for summer, especially now that you're being courted."

"*Courted?* If you're referring to Harrison Blake, you can just forget about that. He and I have about as much in common as lard and water."

Mama again shifted her gaze to the kitchen window. "Do whatever you want, Melissa. Just get on your way before, um, before it gets any hotter. It's going to be a scorcher today."

Mama seems jumpy this morning. Why is she so anxious for me to leave? I still have time to get to the commissary and back before dark. She's up to something!

Melissa kissed her mother on the cheek, picked up her basket, and hurried outside to the barn. She could see Dan already hard at work on the new garden. She wished she had time to talk to him before she left. How nice it would be to share a prayer and a Bible verse to carry with her on the way, but the day ahead loomed long. Instead, she smiled and waved, and Dan returned her greeting.

She hitched Dolly to the buckboard and was about to leave when she heard the sound of approaching horses. If Harrison was calling again, she'd like to get away before he had a chance to talk to her, but with only old Dolly to pull her wagon, there was no hope of that. Instead, she waited in the barn and watched.

Harrison and two of his cowhands rode straight toward her back door. Harrison dismounted and held the reins of his horse, and Mama met him on the steps. "You're early." She spoke in lowered tones, but Melissa could plainly hear her words.

"We've come for him," Harrison said. "We'll make sure you're never troubled by him again. Is he in the barn?"

Melissa's hair stood on end, and her heart banged against the wall of her chest. They had come to get Dan! What did they plan to do with him? How could her mother be a part of such an evil plot? Jumping from the wagon, she slipped around the corner of the barn. "Dan, you've got to hide. Those terrible men are here to get you. Quick, get in the back of my wagon and cover up with that horse blanket. They won't dare search my wagon."

Taken by surprise, Dan was reluctant to put down his hoe. "What terrible men, Melissa? I don't know what you're talking about."

"There's no time for questions." Frantic, Melissa grabbed his hoe and slung it to the ground. "Here, this way." She grabbed him by the arm and pulled him around the back of the barn and through the side door. "Just do as I say. Stay out of sight until I can get rid of them."

Striving to put on a facade of composure, Melissa strode toward the group gathered at her mother's side. "Good morning, Harrison. What brings you out so early?"

Obviously flustered, Harrison looked at Mama. "I thought you said she'd be—"

"Daughter, you might as well know. Harrison is just trying to help. He's promised not to hurt Dan. He just wants to give him a ride through some of these rough woods and put him on the trail to Tallahassee. You said Dan remembered the name of Tallahassee. Maybe when he starts in that direction, he'll remember where he came from."

Melissa had to think of something fast. "Well, that's kindly of you, but you can just save yourselves the trouble. Dan has already left."

"Left?" Harrison's raised eyebrows told Melissa he didn't believe her. "Where did he go?" His cold, steely eyes penetrated her self-control, causing her knees to tremble like a leaf in a windstorm. "Just when did he leave?"

"I. . .He. . ." Recalling the direction of Tallahassee, she pointed west. "He went through the woods that way. Maybe you can catch up with him and give him a ride. I'm sure he would appreciate it." *Forgive me, God.*

"We'll find him, Boss," one of the cowhands said. "With that gimpy leg, he couldn't have gotten far through them woods."

"Perhaps you should all stop for a glass of cool water before you set out. It's going to be very hot today. I'm on my way to Milltown, but I'm sure Mama would be glad to serve you." Melissa could barely tolerate a glance at her mother, but she pasted on her most gracious smile. "They might even enjoy some of that nice orange juice you squeezed this morning, Mama."

Mama twisted her apron in her hands. "Why, yes, certainly. You're all welcome to come in and rest for a spell." She held the kitchen door ajar while all three men tied their horses to the hitching post.

Melissa, ambling toward the barn, called over her shoulder. "I'll be back before dark. Oh, and if you do see Dan, be sure to tell him how much we're going to miss him around here."

Once out of sight, she quickened her pace and took her place in the driver's seat of the old buckboard. "Gee, Dolly." With a flick of the reins, they were off. She didn't stop to contemplate the possible consequences of her actions. She only knew she must get Dan out of the reach of Harrison Blake and his evil cohorts.

Was she wrong to suspect Harrison's motives? But if he truly intended to help Dan, why had he considered it necessary to bring along his henchmen? And to think her own mother would betray her by letting them take Dan away while she was gone!

As she traveled southeast, Melissa cast frequent glances at the reassuring lump beneath the old woolen horse blanket in the back of the wagon. She pressed poor Dolly beyond her endurance, until at last she felt safely cloistered in the thickness of the forest.

Satisfying herself that no one had followed her, she drew the old mare to a halt. As soon as the wagon wheels quit rolling, Dan crawled out of his hiding place and surveyed his surroundings. "What's this all about, Melissa? Where are we?"

"We're no place yet. This is the trail to Milltown. Dan, I'm sorry I didn't have a chance to explain, but I knew I had to get you out of there. Those men knew I wouldn't be home today, and they were planning to take you away before I returned." She climbed down from the wagon to stretch her legs. "We'll have to wait a few minutes while Dolly cools down a little. I'm afraid I pushed her too hard."

Melissa reached over the edge of the buckboard and found a rag to wipe the horse's sweaty flanks. "Poor Dolly. We'll come to the creek soon, and you can have some water." She pulled a burlap sack from the back of the wagon and gave her a handful of oats.

After a brief respite, Melissa climbed back onto the driver's seat, and Dan hopped up to sit beside her. The buckboard bounced forward again, but this time Melissa let Dolly trot along at a leisurely pace.

"Melissa, what do you think this is all about? Do you have any idea what those men planned to do with me?"

Worry lines creased her forehead. "I can only guess. I've wondered myself why Harrison continues to show such an interest in you. He's tried to get his hands on you ever since you first arrived. Do you think it has anything to do with your past?"

"That's the only possible explanation, as far as I can see. He does look familiar. I've never told you about this before, but the other night while you were away, while I was in the kitchen cleaning the stove, two men rode into the backyard on horses branded with a B. I've seen that very same brand on Harrison's horse."

Melissa paled. "What were they planning to do?"

"They were carrying guns, and they were looking for me. I heard one of them say their boss had sent them to get rid of me."

"Oh, Dan, how awful. How did you manage to hide from them?"

"I didn't hide exactly, but I guess it didn't occur to them that I might be inside the house. When they didn't find me in the tack room, they set fire to the corner of your barn and galloped away in a hurry. I had to hustle to extinguish that blaze before it reached the hay and consumed the whole place. That's how I aggravated my ankle."

Melissa was on the verge of tears. She let the reins go slack in her hands. "Why didn't you tell me about this sooner?"

Dan shook his head and rubbed his palms together. "I didn't want to upset you and your mother. I've been far too much trouble for you already. No wonder your ma was willing to let Harrison take me away. I figured if I just up and left on my own, they wouldn't bother you anymore. That's why I'm glad you're getting me away today."

The wagon had come to a standstill, and Dolly nibbled on some of the sparse vegetation that grew at her feet. "Dan, I think I'd better tell you something else before we get there. Have you ever heard of a man named Mr. Whittamore?" She looked at Dan and saw a flash of recognition in his eyes.

"Yes, I think I have. That's a familiar name. Tell me who he is." Dan's voice vibrated with excitement. "Maybe he knows me."

"Mr. Whittamore runs the Milltown commissary." Melissa hoped that, by feeding him clues, Dan could piece everything together and come up with a solution to his identity. "Does that help?"

"I—I'm not sure. What else can you tell me about him?"

Melissa hesitated. Would her secret knowledge about the robbery help Dan remember his past, or would it only add to the heavy burden he carried in his heart? "Actually, there *is* something else. Perhaps I should have told you before now." She looked into his earnest blue eyes and knew she had to tell him the whole story.

fifteen

Dan slumped on the narrow plank seat next to Melissa. "So you're saying I may be the robber they're looking for!"

"Oh no, Dan. You couldn't be the one."

"I can't understand how I could have done such a terrible thing, but if I can't remember anything, how can you be so sure I'm not the one they're looking for?"

Melissa was pained by the stricken look in his eyes. "Because you're a Christian, that's how I'm sure. After all the wonderful things you've taught me about Jesus and His love, I know you couldn't possibly have robbed the commissary."

"I hope you're right." He shifted his weight on the hard wooden seat, still looking unconvinced. "If I've done something wrong, I want to make it right, Melissa, but I'm not going into that commissary with you today. If there's a stigma attached to my past, then I don't want anyone to see us together until I can clear my name. Being associated with me could mean more trouble for you later on."

"But you'll wait outside when I go in?"

"Something like that."

Melissa didn't like the ominous tone of his voice, but she said no more.

They bumped along in silence for a while. Melissa wasn't sure she wanted Dan to confront Mr. Whittamore. Of course Dan wasn't a robber, but what if Mr. Whittamore just *thought* he was. She must find a way to convince Dan to stay outside until she talked to the storekeeper again. Maybe the old gentleman would remember some minor detail that would shed light on the mystery.

Melissa knew of at least one other man in the territory who had blond hair and a wounded right shoulder. Perhaps there were many. It wouldn't be fair to jump to conclusions without knowing all the facts.

Sitting beside her, Dan began to whistle, and Melissa wondered if he was trying to cover up his fears with song. "What is that tune you're whistling?"

"It's a hymn. I know the tune well, and I've been trying to recollect the words. It's something about grace. 'Amazing Grace,' that's it. I wish I could remember all of it." He puckered his lips and began again to whistle.

Melissa thrilled at the quality of his tone. It reminded her of the birds warbling early in the morning. She always wondered what they were singing about, just as she wondered now about Dan and the words that would match his beautiful tune. Picking up the melody, she began to hum along with him. Melissa felt renewed peace and happiness with Dan by her side. If only this contentment could last forever.

As she sighted the commissary in the distance, her heart plummeted to her shoes. No matter what happened today, her time with Dan was drawing to a close.

As if reading her thoughts, Dan stopped whistling and turned to look at her. "Melissa, we both know I can't return to your home with you. For some reason, Harrison Blake is determined to kill me. I'm not afraid for myself as much as I am for you. Those fellows will stop at nothing to accomplish their evil deed, and as long as I'm on your property, you and your mother are in real danger."

A tear slid down Melissa's cheek. "But where will you go?"

Dan lifted his eyes to the heavens. "I'll have the sun by day and the moon by night. The Lord will guide my path, Melissa. We must put our faith in Him."

As soon as Melissa drew the small wagon to a halt outside the store, Dan hopped out and tied Dolly to the hitching post. "Wait out here, Dan. Let me go in first and see what I can find out."

"No, Melissa. You stay with the wagon until I come out. Just remember, if I run into trouble, you're not to acknowledge that you know me. Promise?"

Melissa felt a moment of panic. "I can't promise that."

"That's the way it has to be. If you can't agree to that, then we'll just say good-bye now, and I'll go on my way."

Melissa blanched. Her answer came in a whisper, as more tears slid down her ashen cheeks. "I'll wait."

෨

Walking across the broad wooden walkway fronting the store, Dan had the distinct feeling he had been here before. He opened half of the double screen door and walked inside.

A conversational buzz filled the air, and no one seemed to notice him. *The man behind the counter wearing a white apron must be Mr. Whittamore.* Overhead fans maintained a cool, pleasant atmosphere as Dan circled a pickle barrel and made his way to the counter. "Good afternoon, sir. Are you Mr. Whittamore?" Dan looked at him full in the face and waited for recognition to set in.

Mr. Whittamore gave him an amiable smile. "That's what people call me. What can I do for you?"

"Um, I—I was looking for someone, but I don't see him." Dan continued to stare at the storekeeper, trying hard to remember if they had met before. He turned his face one way and then the other, providing an ample view of his profile, but still the man gave no sign of recognition. A wave of relief swept over Dan. *I'm not a thief! This man acts as though he has never seen me before!*

"Who you be looking for?" Mr. Whittamore asked. "Maybe I can help you. There's been a right smart amount of people in here today."

"I—I don't. . . ," Dan stuttered, trying to come up with a

sensible answer. "Never mind. I don't see him. I guess he isn't here." He turned abruptly before Mr. Whittamore had time to ask more questions.

He made his way to the front door. He must find Melissa and tell her he had passed the first test. She waited anxiously by the wagon, just as she had promised.

He met her worried look with a wide grin. "Good news!"

Melissa drew a sharp intake of breath. "You found out who you are?"

"No, but I found out who I'm *not*. I'm not a thief. Mr. Whittamore didn't know me. I was a total stranger to him. I feel like I've been freed from a great burden."

Seeing her joy at his words made it difficult to speak the words he knew he must say next. "And now, Melissa, it's time for us to say good-bye. I'll never be able to thank you for all you've done for me or to tell you what you've come to mean to me." He reached for her hands, unmindful of the amused stares of people passing by. "I'll never forget you, darling girl. Never."

Melissa's knees wouldn't support her any longer. She slumped down on the hard earth and fought a losing battle with her tears. She buried her face in her hands and sobbed.

Dan knelt down beside her. "Don't cry, Melissa. Someday I'll get my life back together, and when I do, I'll come back to find you."

"No, you won't," she sobbed. "I know I'll never see you again. Oh, Dan, take me with you, please."

"You know I can't do that, Melissa. Not until I have a place for you. But you can do one thing for me."

Melissa lifted her tear-stained face and looked at him through watery eyes. "Anything. I'll do anything to help you."

"Promise you'll pray for me. And keep reading God's Word. Just remember that He has a plan for your life, and if you trust Him, He will show you the way." He took her hands and pulled her to her feet. "Wipe your tears, Melissa, and go into the commissary to get your supplies. I don't want you to watch me leave."

She grabbed her basket from the bed of the wagon and emptied its contents into a gunnysack. "Here, take this. There's a snack I packed for my lunch today and a jar of pickled eggs. There's a bundle of matches in there, too. I always carry some with me in case I have to build a fire. It's not much, but it's all I have to offer."

His attention remained riveted on her face. He slung the sack over his shoulder and used his free left hand to grasp one of hers. "God bless you, Melissa."

She fixed her distraught gaze on his face, trying to embed his features in her memory forever. "I'll pray for you every day, Dan." She pulled her hand from his grasp. "Wait. There's one more thing I want you to have."

Melissa climbed into the bed of the wagon and opened the box that concealed the gun. Pulling off the quilt, she reached in and pulled out her father's rifle. "Here, Dan. You're going to need this more than I will."

Dan backed away, his face registering amazement. "I can't take that, Melissa. That belongs to your family. You might need it."

Ignoring his protest, Melissa thrust the gun into his hands. "Dan, these woods can be dangerous when you go beyond the boundaries of settlements. Outlaws and renegade Indians roam these woods, and wild animals, too. This little snack I'm giving you won't last long, either. You'll have to hunt for food if you're out here very long."

"What will your father say when he finds out you've given away his rifle?"

Melissa didn't want to think about that now. "I'll explain it to him. He'll understand."

Papa would be furious, but she couldn't worry about that.

She squeezed her eyelids to fight back another onslaught of tears, and without a backward glance, she walked slowly toward the store.

❧

Melissa carried her empty basket through the store with a heavy heart. She ambled toward the far corner of the store where bolts of fabric were displayed along the wall. She had no heart for the bright prints today. She was in a gray mood, but gray would never do for Josie Ann's wedding.

"I'll have eight yards of that one," she told the clerk, pointing to a rose-sprigged print she was sure her mother would like. At eighteen cents per yard, it was a costly purchase, but she wanted to make sure she bought enough yardage for a matching bonnet. While the clerk measured and cut, Melissa selected matching thread and a bolt of dainty lace. She was sure Mama would be pleased.

Mama! Would she ever be able to forgive her mother for her terrible deception? Melissa shuddered to think of the possible consequences if she had not been there to help Dan escape. An icy chill ran up her spine.

"Will that be all?" the lady asked.

Melissa had little interest in choosing something for herself. What did it matter? What did anything matter anymore? Then, as though he were standing there beside her, she heard Dan's voice speaking to her heart. *"Just remember that He has a plan for your life, and if you trust Him, He will show you the way."*

She took a deep breath and lifted her chin. "I'll have eight yards of that one," she said, selecting a pale yellow dimity from the shelf. "And a spool of yellow thread."

Walking around the store, picking up the various supplies on Mama's list, Melissa wondered how she could ever get through the rest of the day. Or the rest of her life, for that matter. She had always known that Dan would leave someday, but she hadn't prepared herself for the reality of that someday. Now it was here.

She would pray for him every day, just as she had promised. And she would study the Bible, trying to discover God's plan for her life. Even though the plan could never include Dan, Melissa made a firm resolution that neither would her plan include Harrison Blake. In keeping with the Bible's teachings, she'd have to work hard to forgive her mother's deceitful actions and even harder to stifle her hatred for Harrison Blake.

Melissa took her purchases to the front counter, where Mr. Whittamore stood guard over his money box. She checked the contents of her basket against her list. "I'd like five pounds of those pinto beans, please."

While he measured and weighed her beans, the elderly merchant eyed her critically. "You under the weather today, Sister Malcolm? You're looking a mite peaked."

"No, Mr. Whittamore. I—I guess I'm just a little tired." She didn't feel up to lengthy conversation today, even though her mother would want to hear all the local news when she got home.

"Well, take care of yourself. Better get a bottle of this tonic. The feller who sold it to me said it was good for most anything. I hear there's a lot of malaria going around the territory."

Melissa picked up the bottle to study its label. *Magic Elixir. Cures ague, catarrh, chills, colic, consumption, diarrhea, fever, gout, itch, pinworms, rheumatism. . . .* The list continued on and on. Melissa thought it would truly be magic if this potion lived up to its claims. But she had heard the promises of the patent medicine men before, and she was highly suspicious of their ability to cure anything. "Thank you, Mr. Whittamore, but I believe I'd better just pay you for the things here on the counter." She took out her leather drawstring purse and waited to hear her total.

Mr. Whittamore appeared surprised. "You're paying the whole amount in cash today?"

"Yes, sir. I didn't have anything ready to bring for barter. It was too hot to bring butter, and as for the pickled eggs you like so much, I. . .well, I used them myself."

"Too bad. That's a popular item with the folks around here." He pulled the stub of a pencil from behind his ear and began to cipher on a tablet. He checked his figures before he said, "That'll be seven dollars and sixty-eight cents."

The gold coins rattled on the smooth wood surface of the counter as Melissa counted out the proper total. "There. I believe that is the correct amount. Could you have these put in my wagon for me, please?"

"Certainly." He stashed the money in his box. "I'll have Jonah load this stuff right away, and I thank you kindly for your business. Give my respects to your mama, and tell her I hope she'll be able to come along with you afore long."

"Yes, sir. I'll tell her." Melissa put a few of the smaller items back in her basket and headed for the door.

She was almost to the entrance when she stopped dead in her tracks. A bulletin board hanging on the east wall caught her eye. REWARD! Below that caption, someone had sketched a perfect likeness of Dan. There was no mistaking it. Even the stubborn lock of blond hair hung over his forehead, and his smile revealed a slight separation between his front teeth and two distinct dimples. Yes, unless he had a twin brother, it was definitely a picture of Dan.

Melissa felt faint, and her stomach churned like a volcano ready to erupt. This could not be real! Surely she was living in a nightmare and would wake up at any moment to laugh at herself. Why was Dan a wanted man? What terrible thing had he done? She bumped into customers as she dashed across the room for a closer look.

With an ink-dipped quill, someone had carefully constructed a paragraph beneath the picture: *$100 reward for information on the whereabouts of Don Dupree, beloved son of Carson and Genela Dupree. Last seen on the second day of January 1840.*

Melissa could scarcely take it all in. His name was Don. And he hadn't done any terrible deed. He was simply missing, and he had a loving family who wanted to find him. She hadn't been far off track when she'd named him Dan. Don Dupree! Oh, why couldn't she have seen this sign before he left? At least an hour had passed, and even with his injured ankle, he would have lost himself deep in the woods by now. There was no way she could possibly find him. She wouldn't even know in which direction to start.

Melissa jerked the poster down from the wall and ran back to the front counter. "Mr. Whittamore, I know the man in this picture." Melissa's face, so pale just moments ago when she paid for her supplies, was now covered with a bright scarlet flush. "We've got to find him."

Melissa's shout caused customers to stop what they were doing and gather around her. "What is it, child?" A woman with a baby on her hip eyed her with curiosity. "So you know him? Well, lots of us *know* him, but do you happen to know where he is?"

"Yes—I mean, no! But he was here this morning. He started walking through the woods going east, I think." Melissa wrung her hands. "Oh, we've got to hurry and find him."

Mr. Whittamore had come to stand beside her. "I don't believe Miss Malcolm is well," he told the onlookers. "I thought earlier she was coming down with something. Come over here and sit down, Melissa. You'll feel better after I give you a nice drink of cool water."

"I feel perfectly fine," she insisted. "Don't you understand? Send someone out to look for Dan before he gets hopelessly lost in the woods."

Mr. Whittamore and the lady with the baby exchanged glances. *"Dan?"* The woman stepped forward and tried to console her. "Don't get yourself upset, dearie. I live real close to the Dupree ranch, and I've known Don since he was a toddler. If he's walking in these woods, you don't need to worry. He won't get lost. He knows his way through these woods like the back of his hand."

"But he doesn't remember. . . ."

The woman paid no heed to Melissa's protest. "If it really was Don, his folks will be mighty glad he's finally decided to come home. But most of us figured he was like the prodigal son that took off with the family's fortune. He had his saddlebags filled with gold, and personally, I don't never expect to see him again."

Over her objection, Mr. Whittamore took Melissa by the arm and led her around the corner behind the counter. With a wave of his hand, he dispersed the crowd and sat her on a high stool. As the people wandered off, Melissa overheard several of them clucking to each other. "Poor girl. She's likely suffering from the heat."

Mr. Whittamore took a seat on another stool beside her and began to unfold the story of the poster.

"The Duprees live on a big ranch alongside the Suwannee River. Matter of fact, I don't know any of them except for Carson, the father. Their ranch is a far piece from here, so they don't get up this way much. I reckon they buy their supplies from Joe-Tom's or someplace closer to their homestead. They sent a man up here today, though, just to put up this poster. They're hoping someone around here might recognize him."

Melissa was confused by what she heard. "But why did Dan—er, *Don*—leave home in the first place?"

"Seems as how the family had accumulated a hefty wad of money from some of their cattle drives. It's dangerous to keep a lot of money on hand here in the territory. I know that as well as anyone. Anyway, the Duprees sent their son to the bank in Tallahassee to deliver their gold for safekeeping. They sent another feller, name of Scotty, to go along with him for extra security. When the two fellers didn't get back home after a few weeks, his pa sent all his cow hunters out to look for them."

"And they didn't find either man?"

"They found Scotty's body west of the Fenholloway River. He'd been shot in the head. They searched all through the woods, but didn't find hide nor hair of Don, nor his horse, nor his gold. I reckon they've near about given up hope by now."

"Oh no, they mustn't," Melissa moaned. She tried to tell the elderly merchant about how she had found Dan and nursed him back to health, but she could see by the look on his face that he was highly skeptical of her story.

"Melissa, Jonah has your wagon loaded, and you'd better start back home. You wouldn't want to be out in these parts after dark. It's dangerous enough in the daylight."

"But I need to get word to the Duprees," she wailed. "They have to know their son is alive and lost in the woods."

Mr. Whittamore put his arm around her shoulder and tried to calm her with a pat on the back. "Now, don't you worry your pretty little head about that. I'll make sure somebody gets word to them. But from what the man told me when he brought in the poster, they've had lots of people *think* they saw him, and it always turns out to be somebody else." He walked her out the door and helped her into her wagon.

"But the poster," she protested. "It's him. I know it."

"Honey, there's lots of blond-headed cow hunters in the territory, and most of them look just alike. I even get a mite confused myself when they all come in here together. And as far as the poster goes, it's just a drawing, and sometimes people don't draw so good. If I was you, I'd try to forget about that poster."

Mr. Whittamore, with a concerned expression shadowing his face, helped her climb up into the wagon and waved good-bye.

sixteen

Melissa cried all the way home. She cried for the cruelty of her mother's deception. She cried out of frustration that no one in Milltown wanted to believe her story. She cried from embarrassment, remembering how she had shamelessly begged Dan to take her with him. But most of all, she cried because of her great loss. Dan was gone. Life would never again be the same.

The sun had almost set by the time Melissa reined Dolly into the barn and unhitched the buckboard. Scarcely aware of her hunger and fatigue, she gathered some of her supplies into her basket and trudged toward the back door, unmindful of the dust swirling around her feet.

She dreaded facing Mama. How could she put aside her resentment and forgive her for the things she had done? She whispered a soft prayer for strength and wisdom.

Mama stood on the back steps, waiting to meet her. "I'm glad you're back, Daughter. I've worried about you all day. I know you're vexed with me, but believe me, Melissa, this was for the best. Sooner or later, we knew Dan would have to leave. We couldn't afford to keep him here permanently."

"No, Mama."

"I just didn't expect he'd leave so early like that, without a word to any of us. Harrison and his men rode west looking for him, but they came back around noon and said they didn't find him."

So they hadn't figured out that she took him away in her wagon. *Good!* Let them continue to search the northwest woods for him all they wanted to. Dan was miles away to the southeast, and hopefully he would somehow find his way home. She had done all she could to help him. Now his problems were in God's hands.

"Let's don't talk about it now, Mama. I'm tired. I need to get our things in the house so I can go to the barn and milk Flossie." She brushed past her mother and went into the kitchen.

Mama followed her. "Honey, are you still mad at me?"

Melissa shook her head. She tried to deny her feelings, but the words just wouldn't come out.

"I only did what was best for all of us—Dan, too," Mama persisted. "I declare, that Harrison Blake is such a kind man. A girl would be mighty lucky to make a catch like that. He feels sorry for Dan and wants to help him get back to wherever it is he's going. I told them Dan remembered something about Tallahassee. If he's headed that way, Harrison said his cow hunters will likely find him."

Melissa stifled a smile, the first to tease her lips since morning. She pictured Harrison and his men scouring the west woods, futilely searching for a man who was far, far away in the opposite direction.

Melissa poured water into a basin and picked up a square of lye soap to wash her hands. "There's still enough light for milking if I hurry." She slid the milk pail from the shelf and kissed her mother on the cheek—a gesture that spoke of love and forgiveness. What was done was done. There was no need to sulk and argue about what was now behind them. She let the back door slam in her wake as she made her way across the sandy yard in the fading light of day.

⋙

Afternoon sunlight filtered through the dense forest, painting slashes of gold across the pine-needle floor. Dan's intuition told him that with each step, he moved closer to home. But at the same time, he couldn't erase from his mind the knowledge that each step moved him farther away from Melissa.

Darling Melissa! How had he come to care so deeply for her in such a short time? He didn't deserve the right to love her, especially since he had nothing of his own to offer. Perhaps in time he would find a place for himself in this world, but by then, Melissa would probably have already pledged her life to Harrison Blake.

The very thought of Harrison laying a hand on Melissa's innocent beauty fueled a fire in Dan's belly like a stick of dynamite. What was there about that man that raised his hackles and fueled his anger? Why was Dan so sure that Harrison was the one who wanted him dead? His feeling was based on more than the conversation he had overheard the night Harrison's henchmen had tried to burn down the barn. Dan was sure his reaction went back much further, to some hazy memory in his past. If only he could bring the details into focus.

His throat felt parched and dry, and his stomach began to rumble, reminding him that he hadn't eaten anything all day. Anxious to put some space between himself and anyone who might come looking for him, Dan had walked at a brisk pace for several hours. He had studiously avoided signs of trails, preferring to secrete himself among the sheltering shadows of oaks and pines. But now, deep in the woods, he felt securely out of touch with the rest of the world.

As he walked, he prayed. "Lord, I don't know where I'm headed, but I'm putting myself in Your care. If I have a home out there somewhere, I'm trusting You to show me the way."

He began to look for a smooth place on which to rest, but seeing none, he plowed onward. In the distance, he thought he heard a soft rustle, and he began to move toward the sound of what he perceived to be running water. As he continued, the soft rustle escalated gradually into a steady roar. *Water!* He was sure of it.

Dan quickened his steps. His thirst was even more severe than his hunger. He wove his way around the thick trees until at last a broad, rocky creek came into view.

Thank You, Lord! Dan knelt beside the water's edge and used his hands to scoop up cool, fresh water. After he slaked his thirst, he splashed his face and hands from the refreshing stream, letting its wetness trickle down the front of his shirt. His relief was so great that he laughed aloud.

Spotting a large limestone boulder along the creek bank, he sat on its flat surface and slid the rifle and gunnysack from his shoulders. He opened the package of lunch that Melissa had given him—a lunch she had prepared for herself. He pictured her at the kitchen table early this morning, putting it all together with her beautiful hands. He bowed his head and gave thanks, adding, "Lord, please guide my steps, and watch over Melissa and keep her safe."

Inside the package he discovered two thick buttermilk biscuits, sliced and filled with thin, sweet slices of smoked ham. Three chunky oatmeal cookies, generously laced with broken bits of pecan meats, were wrapped in a square of gingham. And, of course, there was a whole jar of Mrs. Malcolm's delicious eggs pickled in limewater. He rationed out two for his supper, knowing that when this food was gone, he would be forced to live off the land by the skill of his hands.

While he ate, he studied the movement of the creek. Chestnut Creek! It came to him in a flash. And Chestnut Creek emptied into the Suwannee River! How did he know all this? His heart began to pound fiercely in his chest. This little piece of information was a jewel in his collection of memories because he was quite certain he had ties to the Suwannee River. He would follow this stream to its end, but in which direction should he begin?

❧

Melissa sat at the kitchen table, reading God's Word by the

light of a lard-oil lantern. Dan had been gone for over a week. Oh, how she missed him. With no one to explain their meanings to her, Melissa found some of the verses puzzling and difficult to understand. Gingerly she turned the thin, yellowed pages of Granny's Bible and pored over the small black print. "Listen to this, Mama. Sit down and let me read this to you."

"I don't have time for reading, Melissa, and neither do you. I've got this floor to mop, and there's all that cream in the springhouse waiting to be churned into butter. I declare, you do waste a lot of time lately." But Melissa noted that in spite of her words, Mama peered over her shoulder, trying to catch a glimpse of the precious text.

Encouraged by her morsel of interest, Melissa began to read aloud. " 'Come unto me, all ye that labour and are heavy laden, and I will give you rest.' "

"Well, that sounds like it's talking about me all right," Mama grunted. "I'm heavy laden for sure, but I don't see as how that Jesus of yours can give me any rest."

Melissa wished that Dan were here to explain salvation to Mama the way he had outlined it for her. She said a silent prayer that God would give her the right words to open the door of her mother's heart.

"Just for a few minutes, Mama. Sit here with me, and I'll mop the floor for you later so you can go to bed."

With one hand, Mama rubbed the muscles in her left hip and drew in a deep breath. Visible weariness hovered over her like a heavy cloud. Melissa watched her battle with the temptation to rest.

"Come on," Melissa coaxed, scooting over and drawing in her skirts to make room on the bench. With a sigh, Mama leaned the mop against the wall and parked herself beside her daughter at the kitchen table.

Melissa had used small scraps of paper to mark some of

her favorite passages. She turned to one of them and began to read.

" 'For God so loved the world, that he gave his only begotten Son, that whosoever believeth in him should not perish, but have everlasting life.'

"Isn't that exciting, Mama? You see, God is not just for rich people like you thought. His words are a free gift for everyone who will accept them. Dan helped me to understand this. God loved us so much that He sent His only Son to suffer and die on the cross, so that anybody who believes in Him can be forgiven of their sins and live with Him forever."

Melissa waited for the argument she was sure would follow from her mother's lips, but oddly, none came. Mama sat in thoughtful silence, her elbows propped on the table and her head held tightly between both hands. What was she thinking? Melissa was hesitant to break into her thoughts with words.

If Dan were here, he would know just how to use this moment to lead Mama into the beautiful experience of salvation. But he *wasn't* here, not now or ever. It was up to Melissa to do the best she could and trust Jesus to do the rest.

Slipping an arm around her mother's shoulder, she whispered, "Mama, wouldn't you like to give your heart to Jesus right here and now and know you'll live in heaven with Him forever?"

Mama furrowed her brow and shook her head. "I'll admit it sounds good when you talk about it, but I just don't think I can do it. In the first place, I don't know how. And look at me. I'm nobody special—just an ordinary country woman."

Melissa flipped the pages to another of her specially marked passages and read, " 'If any man be in Christ, he is a new creature: old things are passed away; behold, all things are become new.' I can help you, Mama, if you're ready."

Mama rubbed her forehead. "Aren't we supposed to be in a church or somewhere special to do this?"

Melissa twisted her body to face her mother, reaching out to grasp her hands. "Any place at all will do just fine. Jesus has promised to be with us always, no matter where we are."

Melissa began to lead her mother in the prayer Dan had taught her, asking God's forgiveness for sins and accepting God's free gift of salvation. Mama, her eyes gently closed, repeated the words after her. At the final *amen,* the two women lifted their faces and smiled at each other, their eyes glistening with unshed tears. Then, without speaking a word, they fell into each other's arms, sharing a long, warm embrace.

The blue flame sputtered and died, consuming the last bit of oil in the rusty old lantern, plunging the little house in the woods into peaceful darkness.

seventeen

Melissa sat on her milking stool, softly humming the tune she had memorized by listening to Dan's melodic whistling on the day she had driven him to Milltown.

She wished she knew the words to his haunting song. Dan said it was something about amazing grace. As she hummed, she could almost imagine Dan sitting beside her, trilling his sweet notes in her ear. The beat of her song was punctuated by rhythmic pings, as Flossie's warm milk hit the metal pail in sporadic streams.

When she could no longer coax out any more milk, Melissa thanked Flossie by affectionately rubbing her between her ears. She picked up her bucket and carried it into the house, still humming the wordless melody.

Mama sat in the rocking chair, sewing lace onto her new summer dress. "I'm nearly done with yours, too, Daughter. I'll need for you to try it on so I can mark the hem, and then you can mark mine for me."

"It's turning out real pretty, Mama. You'll be the prettiest lady at the wedding."

Mama blushed and smiled. "Oh, get on with you. I'm just an old woman now, but I have to admit I did draw a bit of attention from the fellows when I was your age." Her needle stopped, and her eyes took on a dreamy look. "I met your papa at a church picnic one afternoon, and he took a shine to me right away."

Melissa poured the fresh milk into clean glass jars, ready to transfer to the springhouse. "I bet he did, Mama. I've heard him talk about how your golden curls caught his eye."

Mama smiled, but then her expression sobered. "Melissa, while we're on the subject. . ."

Oh no! Not that again! Melissa knew what was coming next. Even though Mama had changed since she accepted Jesus in her heart, there was one thing she refused to change. She seemed more determined than ever that her daughter should marry Harrison Blake.

"You have an opportunity that many girls your age would envy. Harrison Blake is the most successful rancher in these parts, honey, and he wants you to be his wife."

"But, Mama, I've told you before. I don't love Harrison, and I am not going to marry him."

Mama shook her head. "It was all right to dream about love when you were sixteen, Melissa, but you're twenty years old now. It's time you put away your foolishness. Harrison is what you could call a real catch, and I don't know how much longer he's going to be patient with you. If you turn him away now, some other lucky girl will be more prudent, and you could end up spending the rest of your life a *spinster*." Mama spit out that last word like an insipid dose of castor oil.

Melissa did not tell her mother that she would much prefer spinsterhood to spending her life with a man she did not love, especially if that man were Harrison Blake. But realizing through experience that arguments on this subject were useless, she picked up the jars of fresh milk and took them to the springhouse.

&

Dan opened his eyes and squinted into the morning sun. His small fire smoldered by the creek bank. With the approach of summer, the nights were warmer, but Dan always made a fire beside his bed at night to repel the wild animals that roamed the Florida woods.

Several times he had heard hungry wolves howling in the dark, and he sometimes caught a glint of unidentified eyes curiously peering at him through the bushes. As long as they didn't threaten him, he was content to leave them alone. Although he kept his rifle by his side at all times, he was careful not to waste his small supply of ammunition.

After his hoard of pickled eggs was gone, Dan subdued his hunger with wild nuts and berries, and once he had shot an armadillo for his evening meal. It didn't taste like steak, but it served to quiet his rumbling stomach.

Following the winding path of Chestnut Creek, Dan always had an ample supply of water. Many times each day, he scooped it up with cupped hands to satisfy his thirst, and he often wished he could jump in to bathe himself in the clear, crystal stream. He had abandoned that idea on the day he saw two alligators battling over the remains of a snapping turtle. Those giant jaws would relish a man Dan's size. He could imagine them fighting over his body, a much greater prize than that poor old turtle.

Dan covered the smoldering embers with sand and slung his gunnysack and rifle over his shoulder. Thanks to the excellent care of Melissa and her mother, his wounds had almost completely healed. He walked without the aid of a stick, and thankfully he had regained the full use of his right arm.

He prayed daily for Melissa and for Mrs. Malcolm, too. Without their kindness, he would likely be dead by now. He hoped Mr. Malcolm would soon return home to care for his precious family. The Florida Territory was not a safe place for two women living alone.

Absorbed in his thoughts, Dan kept up a brisk pace along the bank of the creek. Surely he would find the Suwannee River soon, unless he was traveling in the wrong direction. He had seen no signs of human life since leaving Milltown. Of course, he had only himself to blame for that. Had he chosen to follow the trail, things might have been different. But with Blake and his gang trying to find him, he was sure he had made the right decision by cutting through the densest part of the forest.

As the sun climbed higher in the sky, Dan began to wither in the heat, and rivulets of perspiration streamed down his face. He placed his sack and gun on the ground and slid down the creek bank to enjoy a drink of water before continuing on his way.

The cool water trickled down his throat, and he welcomed the excess that dribbled down his chin and inside the neck of his shirt.

As he turned to make his way back up the bank, he was startled to see a bearded old man looking down at him. The rifle he held in his wrinkled hands was the one Dan had carelessly left on the ground. It was aimed directly at him. Helpless to defend himself, Dan held his arms high in the air.

"Who be you?" the grizzled old man asked. His voice was raspy, and his cheek bulged with what Dan supposed to be a wad of chewing tobacco.

"I–I'm Dan." That was as close as he could come to the truth. He didn't think it wise to admit he didn't know his own identity, especially while he was looking down the barrel of a loaded rifle.

"Get up here and let me look at you. And don't try nothin' foolish."

Dan scrambled up the bank and stood six feet in front of the old man. He looked feeble and would be no match for Dan except for the weapon he held in his hands.

"I don't have any money," Dan said. "All I have is what you see there on the ground, but you're welcome to whatever I have."

"I ain't no outlaw, sonny." The old geezer lowered the gun but kept a firm grip on its handle. "A body has got to be mighty keerful around here. Can't never tell what a stranger has got on his mind. What you be doin' in these here parts?"

Dan felt a surge of relief. If it was true that his newfound companion meant no harm, there was a chance he might even turn out to be helpful. "I'm lost, sir. I'm trying to follow this creek to the Suwannee. Can you tell me how much farther it is?" Dan had a wild fear that the man might tell him he had been traveling in the wrong direction, but instead, he lifted a bony finger and pointed to the east. " 'Bout two days from here. Course you probably walk faster than an old man like me, so maybe a day and a half for you." The man squinted as he eyed Dan from head to toe. "How long since you et, sonny?"

"Um, I had supper last night, but I haven't stopped to fix anything this morning. I wanted to get a good start before it got too hot." Dan wanted his rifle back, but he was reluctant to antagonize the man by asking. "Sir, do you live around here? What is your name?"

The man spat, sending a dark stream of tobacco juice down the creek bank. "Name's Luke. I got me a shanty through the woods yonder. I just come down here to fill my bucket with water when I seen you. I don't want no trouble."

"I mean you no harm. If you'll. . .um. . .return my rifle, I'll be on my way."

"Not so fast," Luke said, drawing back and tightening his grip on the gun. "I've gotta cogitate about this a mite." After a thoughtful pause, he asked, "What's in that-there knapsack?"

"There's not much left," Dan told him. "I've still got a few matches, but they don't work too good anymore. I've tried to keep them dry, but the night air and the morning dew have just about ruined them. Say, you wouldn't have a couple you could spare, would you?"

Luke scratched his gray beard with his free hand. "I might." He stared at Dan, apparently sizing him up before he reached a decision. He was silent for so long that Dan began to believe he had received all the answer he was going to get. He was itchy to get on his way, but he really needed his gun; and if Luke could spare a few matches, that would be a real plus.

At last the old-timer broke the silence. "Tell you what. You walk back to the shanty with me, and I'll fry us up some catfish. We can sit down and talk things over. I'll be thinkin' about them matches and about this-here rifle, too."

Dan had little choice but to follow him, although he had no idea what kind of trouble he might be getting into.

&

As spring melded into summer, the days grew longer, giving Melissa more daylight hours in which to do her chores. For this she was grateful, because she and Mama now began each day by reading and studying God's Word. Just as the Bible promised, Mama was truly a different person since she had given her heart to the Lord.

But there was one thing about her mother that had not changed at all. She seemed more determined than ever that her daughter should marry Harrison Blake. Yesterday, when he stopped by to give them some tomatoes from his garden, he had promised to return today with a loin of pork for their table. Melissa wished she could hide somewhere and let Mama entertain him when he arrived.

Mama was beside herself with joy over the gifts Harrison continued to bestow on her daughter. "I hope you'll be nice to him today, Melissa. I should think you'd be happy to see him. He's keeping our food cupboard so well supplied, you haven't needed to go to the commissary in weeks."

Melissa had learned long ago that it was best not to comment whenever Mama's opinions differed from her own. Admittedly, Mama's appetite had greatly improved with Harrison's additions to their table, and Melissa was pleased to see the rosy glow returning to her cheeks. But as for herself, she almost choked on the food sometimes when she stopped to realize the strings attached to their good fortune. She wasn't *that* hungry yet.

Melissa was busy hanging her wash on the line when she heard the sound of an approaching horse. She sighed. It must surely be Harrison. It couldn't be anyone else.

"Melissa," her mother called from the back door. "Honey, come in and pretty yourself up. Your beau is coming."

"I don't have a beau, Mama, and I'm too busy to stop what I'm doing right now, if I expect this wash to get dry before dark. If anyone needs to see me, I'll be out here under the clothesline."

She stooped to pick up one of Mama's muslin aprons from her laundry basket and hung it on the line. She had just picked up a wet dress, focusing her attention on her work, when her mother's shriek pierced the air. She dropped the dress in the dirt and ran toward the house to see what had happened. Taking the back steps two at a time, she jerked open the screen door. "What. . . ?"

There in the kitchen stood Papa, lifting Mama off her feet and twirling her around in a circle. Mama was shrieking and giggling like a schoolgirl.

"Papa! You're home!" Melissa was so excited to have Papa home again that she failed to notice Harrison standing in the doorway, observing the scenario unfolding in the little kitchen.

"I'll get out of your way here and let you enjoy this happy reunion," Harrison said, drawing the attention of all three members of the Malcolm family.

Papa took a step forward and stretched out his hand. "Thank you again, Harrison. If you hadn't come along when you did, I wouldn't have made it home before dusk." Turning to the two women, he explained, "There was an accident in the Okefenokee where my crew was working, and we all got laid off for a few weeks. I hitched a ride on a logging truck coming this way and rode south until they turned west. Then I got off and started walking the rest of the way home. Lucky for me, Harrison here came along and brought me the rest of the way on the back of his horse. I'm much obliged to you, Harrison."

"Glad I could help, sir. Actually, I was on my way over here anyway to deliver this pork." He laid a neatly wrapped package on the kitchen table. "Melissa, perhaps you'd do me a great honor by walking with me to the gate."

Melissa's cheeks burned. She cast a pleading look at her father. "Well, I. . ."

"Of course she will," Papa said, beaming a smile and a wink in Melissa's direction. "Don't linger out there too long, honey. I know you and Harrison have a lot to talk about these days, but I want some time with you, too."

Her disappointment hung like a weight in her chest. Didn't Harrison realize this was a special time when she wanted to be with her family? Resigned to her fate, she whispered, "I won't be long."

When Harrison reached for her arm, Melissa dodged his touch and preceded him out the front door. She kept two steps ahead of him all the way to the gate. "Thank you for the meat, Harrison. I'm sure we'll enjoy it."

Harrison gripped her wrists in his massive hands and held tight. "Melissa, you have gone out of your way to avoid me, but this time you are going to stay here and listen to what I have to say."

Melissa tried to twist free of his grasp. "You're hurting my arms."

"I'm sorry," he said, but he did not release her. "I'm glad I had a chance to visit with your father. He and I had quite an interesting talk, and most of it involved you." Towering over her, he kept his eyes fixed on her face as he spoke. "I'm sure it won't come as any surprise to you to learn that I've offered to marry you."

"*Offered?*" Melissa's emotions concerning Harrison had run

the gamut from fear to a simple distaste, but now what she felt was anger. How dare he come here and act as though she would consider herself lucky and fall into his arms! "Whatever happened to *asking*? Am I to have no say in this matter?"

"Grow up, Melissa. You need to understand a few things. Don't you realize that after you marry me, your whole life will change from poverty to luxury?"

"I like my life just as it is, thank you." Her temper boiled within her like a pot of beef stew. "I can't marry you, Harrison. I don't love you, and if the truth be told, you don't love me, either."

"Foolish girl," Harrison hissed through white lips. "What do you know of love? Love has nothing to do with my proposal of marriage. The fact is, I'm not getting any younger, and I would like to have a son to carry on my name after I'm gone. And another thing, I entertain often, and I need someone to sit at my table and serve as hostess."

"So what you're looking for is a housekeeper and a nanny, is that it?"

Harrison mellowed his tone. "Melissa, listen to me. I will leave you with this thought. I don't deny that I find you quite attractive, but I am not a patient man. You are not the only pretty girl in the territory, and I don't plan to play games to get what I want. I suggest you go inside and talk to your parents. I'll expect an answer within the week."

At last Melissa was able to wrench herself free. Her wrists were red from his tight hold on her. "Thank you for your generous *offer*, Harrison. And now I want to get back and visit with my papa. He's been gone a very long time."

She turned and walked up the path to her front steps. Her legs shook so badly that she wondered how she could make it all the way back to the house. *What arrogance!* She could imagine few things worse than spending the rest of her life married to such a man!

eighteen

Luke rolled thin fillets of catfish in cornmeal before sliding them into the melted lard sizzling in his cast-iron spider. Dan, his salivary glands aroused by the delicious aroma, watched him moisten the remaining cornmeal and roll it into walnut-sized balls. As soon as the catfish came out of the pan, Luke dropped the wads of cornmeal into the hot grease. "You like hush puppies?" He flipped them over the coals of an open fire.

Dan tried to remember. The word had a familiar ring. "Yes. . .yes, I believe I do."

Luke raised his eyebrows and gave Dan a quizzical stare. Dan realized he needed to be more careful in the way he phrased his comments. "I really do like them," he repeated with forced enthusiasm.

Luke divided the food onto two tin plates and handed one to Dan. "You a prayin' man?"

His question caught Dan by surprise. "Why, yes, I am." Could it be his good fortune to have fallen into the hands of a Christian man?

"You wouldn't just be tellin' me that so's I'd trust you, would you? 'Cause I still ain't made up my mind about you yet."

Dan thought actions might speak louder than words. "Sir, would you like for me to return thanks before we eat?"

Luke's guarded glare was a sure sign of his suspicions about his visitor, but when he nodded, Dan bowed his head and began to pray. "Dear Lord, I thank You for my new friend and for the food we are about to share. Lord, I thank You for bringing the two of us together. Help us to build a true friendship based on trust in You and in each other. In Jesus' name we pray. Amen."

Luke echoed the "Amen." As he began to eat, Dan could sense the old man's growing ease. He suspected the change was due to their kinship through Christ. Surely the Lord had brought him to this place.

"Where'd you say you was goin'?" Luke asked, removing a fish bone from his mouth and using it to pick a morsel of food from his teeth.

With his mouth full of hush puppies, Dan mumbled, "Home. I'm going home." He hoped his new friend would let the matter drop there. He didn't want to be faced with a lot of questions he couldn't answer. He was grateful to Luke for the first real meal he had enjoyed since leaving the Malcolms' homestead, but he wanted to get his hands on that rifle and move on.

In an effort to change the subject, Dan eyed his humble surroundings. "Luke, what do you do for a living?"

Luke wiped greasy fingers on his britches. "It don't take much to keep me goin'. I do a little trappin' and huntin' now and then, just enough to barter for my supplies. I used to be a bounty hunter, but I got too old for that." Dan saw a light in Luke's rheumy eyes as a new hope seemed to emerge in his mind. "Say, sonny," he said, scrutinizing Dan anew, "is anybody lookin' fer *you*?"

"If you mean, am I wanted for some crime, the answer is no. Luke, I'm much obliged to you for your hospitality, but if you'll return my rifle, I'll go on and get out of your way."

The possibility of a reward had put new life into the old man. "I believe I'll walk along with you to the Suwannee. We can stop in at the general store and check things out. If you be what you say, I'll give you your gun and some matches, too. But I reckon I'll just hold onto this thing till we make sure."

Inwardly, Dan groaned. Traveling two days with his aged friend would surely slow down his progress, just when he had begun to sense he was almost home. He was twice the size of Luke, and he could easily wrestle the gun from him; but he didn't want to hurt the old man. "All right, but let's get going. You said it's two days away, and half of this day is already gone."

Luke seemed in no hurry as he rose from the table and began to throw a few supplies in a faded knapsack. "I got all the time in the world, sonny." He cackled at his own humor. "And a *ree-ward* would come in mighty handy, it would."

&

"What do you mean, you gave away my rifle? Melissa, are you completely daft?" Melissa had seldom seen Papa as angry as he was at this moment. "I thought I could leave you in charge of things while I was gone, but I can see I made a big mistake."

"I'm sorry, Papa." But Melissa knew that, under the circumstances, she would do the same thing again. "I couldn't let Dan set off in the woods alone with no way to protect himself. He needed that gun more than we did." A river of tears streamed down her cheeks.

"He needn't have set off alone," Papa argued. "From what your mother has told me, Harrison was kind enough to offer his help in getting the man relocated."

"Harrison and his men didn't want to help Dan. They wanted to kill him. They even tried to burn down our barn one night just to get rid of him," Melissa begged her father to understand.

"You don't know that, and I for one doubt it. Why would Harrison care a fig about an itinerant who was taking shelter in our barn, except for your own protection? I think that hobo was spinning tales, trying to gain your sympathy, and evidently, it worked."

Papa paced the floor while Mama stood quietly in the

corner, wringing her hands. "Don't you see the position this has put me in?" he asked. "We can't live out here on this wild frontier without a gun, and I don't have enough money to buy a replacement." His voice escalated with each sentence, until at last he seemed to have run out of steam. He shook his head and drew in a deep breath of resignation. "I'll just have to see if I can borrow a rifle from Harrison until I can afford a new one. I suppose he'll lend me one. After all, he's like part of our family now."

All the blood drained from Melissa's face. "Family? Papa, please don't keep thinking I'm going to marry Harrison Blake, because I'm not. I've tried to explain to you and Mama that I don't love him."

"Daughter, you've been reading too many of those silly magazine stories your friend Josie Ann gives you. I want you to stop reading those things. You'd do better to spend your time reading the *Farmers' Almanac* and learning about the real world."

"Papa, that brings up another matter I've been hoping to talk to you about. Mama and I have been reading something more important and exciting than either of those."

"More important than the *Farmers' Almanac*? I can't imagine what that could be. If Josie Ann is filling up your head with more—"

"We've been reading Granny's Bible, Papa. And we've both given our hearts to Jesus. Oh, Papa, I can't begin to tell you how wonderful He is and how our lives have changed since we made that decision." She prayed with all her heart that Papa would at least give her a chance to explain, so that he, too, could claim the wonderful promise of eternal life.

Momentarily stunned, Papa looked from his wife to his daughter, seeking a denial from either of them. Receiving none, he continued to stride back and forth across the narrow room.

"Papa, if you'll let us explain it to you, I think you. . ."

Papa stopped pacing long enough to stare into Melissa's eyes and point a finger at her nose. "Young lady, it's high time you thought about somebody besides yourself for a change."

Melissa could barely find her voice. "What do you mean, Papa?"

"Think about this. When you marry Harrison, he is going to give me a job on his ranch. I won't have to go away and leave you two women alone to take care of yourselves, and I can certainly see by your recent behavior that you're incapable of doing that. What's more, as part of Harrison's family, we'll always have plenty of food on our table, and you can have as many new dresses as you want. Love is something that will come later. Daughter, you can make all this happen if you try."

"I don't want new dresses," Melissa protested, "and we always manage to have enough food to—"

"Enough! I refuse to discuss this further. Besides, I've already given Harrison my word that you will marry him, and I never break a promise. Now, I suggest you put aside your foolishness and get busy planning your wedding. Harrison thinks we should get on with it as soon as possible."

Melissa retreated to the sanctity of her room, but her sobs carried beyond the closed door. Why hadn't Mama risen to her defense? With Dan gone, she now had only one source of refuge. She picked up her Bible from the table next to her bed, opened the pages, and began to read.

nineteen

Although Luke directed their path along the side of the creek, he insisted that Dan walk several yards ahead of him. Luke knew the woodland trails like an Indian scout, and often as the creek wound in wide curves, he showed Dan how to take shortcuts through the trees, crossing back and forth across the rocky swirls in places where the water narrowed.

Dan carried two knapsacks because Luke insisted on toting two rifles—Dan's and one of his own. Dan supposed Luke brought the extra gun to use on his trip back home, in case he decided to return the one he had taken from Dan.

As evening approached, the men selected a spot and raked a clearing for their campsite. Luke sent Dan to gather wood for their campfire while he took both rifles and went in search of some meat for their supper.

Fallen limbs were everywhere, but the challenge for Dan came in trying to find broken pieces small enough for their fire. The last thing either of them wanted was to start a fire that could quickly grow out of control here in the middle of the dry, dense Florida woods.

Finally, his arms laden with branches, Dan started back toward their camp. He heard a crackle of limbs and caught a glimpse of movement between the trees. "Is that you, Luke?" He stood still and waited for an answer.

Seemingly from out of nowhere, an enormous black bear blocked his path. Without a gun, Dan was defenseless. He stood perfectly still, his heart hammering against the walls of his chest. When the bear moved two steps closer and bared its teeth, Dan thought this was sure to be his last day on earth. *Lord Jesus, please help me!*

Without warning, a shot exploded in the still evening air. The bear hurled around, gave an angry growl, and scampered away through the trees. Only then did Luke emerge from behind a giant oak, the barrel of his rifle still smoking.

"That was a close one," he chortled. "We better get that fire started afore it gets any darker. This is the time of day when the critters start to come out. They'll come this way lookin' for water."

Dan struggled to regain his breath. "Thanks, Luke. It's a good thing you came along when you did. That bear planned on having me for supper."

Luke laughed. "Maybe not. He probably just wanted to see who was trespassin' on his land."

Dan rummaged in his knapsack and retrieved the precious bundle of matches Melissa had insisted on giving him when he left. "I'll get the fire going right now," he volunteered. "I don't want any more encounters with wild animals."

"I got us a rabbit all skinned and ready to roast," Luke boasted, holding his treasure aloft. He watched the fire spring to life under Dan's direction.

After a satisfying supper of roasted rabbit and boiled coffee, the two men used their hands to rake pine needles into mounds, assembling makeshift beds to protect their bodies from the hard ground. "You reckon you killed that bear?" Dan asked, looking warily over his shoulder.

"Naw. His hide is so tough, it would take a bigger bullet than I've got to kill that old scoundrel. I just insulted him, but he'll get over it, and he'll likely be back before the night is over."

Dan squirmed on his prickly bed. A panther screeched in the distance, and an owl hooted from his lofty abode, reminding Dan that *he* was the one who was the intruder here.

His nightly prayer always contained a petition to help him

regain his memory and to find the way home. He was getting closer every day. He could feel it. His excitement mounted. What would home be like, and who would be waiting for him there?

His last thoughts before falling asleep were of Melissa. He could imagine her standing beside him, her hair glistening in the moonlight. No matter what he discovered when he eventually found his way home, one thing he knew for certain: For the rest of his life and into eternity, he would always love Melissa Malcolm with all his heart. He wished he could have told her so.

❧

Melissa watched her mother sew lace edging onto the ruffles of her new white organdy dress, the dress designed to be her wedding gown.

Melissa fought back the tears welling beneath her eyelids. Josie Ann continued to radiate happiness over her wedding plans. Why couldn't she, Melissa, claim any of that happiness for herself? Weren't brides supposed to be happy?

Papa had gone out of his way to be kind to her since the date had been set. Melissa would have been less dejected if the planned festivities were for her funeral instead of her wedding.

Questions swirled in her troubled mind. Why hadn't Dan taken her away with him when he left? Why didn't anyone ever ask her what *she* wanted? And finally, if God had a plan for her life, how would she ever find it if she was forced to marry a man whom she did not love—a man she believed to be cruel and unkind? She prayed daily for guidance, but sometimes she felt as though even Jesus Himself had deserted her.

"And, lo, I am with you always!" The words projected themselves on her heart at the times when she needed them most. Again and again, she turned to her Bible for answers.

Melissa took full advantage of her father's recent desire to placate her. Papa now tolerated the morning devotions of his wife and daughter, even though he still refused to take part in them. But as the three of them sat at their table each morning, reading from God's Holy Word, Melissa thought she detected a spark of interest growing in her father's eyes. *One day,* she thought. *One day he will give his heart to the Lord, and on that day, there will be great rejoicing in heaven, just as the Bible promises.*

Mama rearranged the voluminous gown in her lap. "Look, Melissa. I'll have this ready for you to try on by tomorrow." She held it up by the shoulder seams. "Isn't it lovely? Harrison is going to be absolutely spellbound when he sees you in this."

At the mention of her fiancé's name, Melissa gave an involuntary shudder. "I'm going outside to work in the garden, Mama. I'll be back directly."

"Your papa said you didn't need to work in the garden while he's home, Melissa. He said he'd take care of it. He wants to spare your hands so they'll be smooth and pretty for your wedding day. Why don't you get out your embroidery and make something for your trousseau?"

"Later, Mama." Melissa headed for the backyard. The only thing she could hope for at this point was a reprieve—a miracle. Maybe the circuit rider would be delayed, and they would have to postpone the wedding.

Harrison had suggested hiring a magistrate out of Tallahassee to come and perform the ceremony in his elegant drawing room. Melissa, however, had held firm in her determination to be married by a man of the cloth.

"But that could take weeks," Harrison protested. "What difference does it make who reads the words, as long as the marriage is legal?"

Although Papa agreed with Harrison's opinion, he gave in to Melissa's demands. "If it's that important to her, a few weeks can't make that much difference."

Melissa knew she held the upper hand with Papa until after the wedding. She had to make the most of it while she could, knowing that once she said, "I do," her opinions would no longer make a difference. "I want to be married by a preacher, and I want to be married in my own home."

"But, honey, we don't have room for a lot of people," Mama protested. "Just think what a stylish affair it would be in the Blakes' spacious home."

But Melissa remained firm. "If we don't have enough room inside, we'll have it outside underneath the trees," she said. Given a few more weeks, maybe a miracle would occur. Maybe Harrison would have a change of heart and find someone else more suitable for his lifestyle, or maybe Papa would see that the whole idea was one giant mistake. In any case, she was grateful for the short reprieve.

She found a hoe in the barn and set out for the garden plot. She loved working with the tender new plants sprouting in the patch of earth Dan had tilled for her. She stooped to pull a few weeds encroaching on her tomato plants.

Dan! How she missed him! She tried to imagine him finding his way home to a loving family, his memory fully restored. Mr. Whittamore had promised to notify his parents of his whereabouts. Surely they would have sent out a search party to find him by now and return him to his home. Would he ever think of her and remember the intimate thoughts they had shared?

No matter how much she loved him—and yes, she had finally admitted to herself that she did indeed love him—she must work to put him out of her mind forever. In just a few short weeks, she'd be a married woman, married to a man she would never love but to whom she would be faithful for the rest of her life.

Papa said love would come after she married Harrison

Blake, but Melissa knew otherwise. Yet once she took her marriage vows, she would honor them according to the words of scripture. And she could take joy in knowing that life for her parents would be easier, and Papa would never have to leave home again.

She hoed to the rhythm of the song in her heart, humming the melody Dan had whistled on their last day together. "Amazing Grace"! Perhaps someday she would learn the words, but for now she was happy to hum the haunting melody that brought memories of her secret love and snuggled them in her heart.

twenty

"Just how much farther is this general store you keep telling me about?" Dan looked at the darkening sky. "Do you think we'll get there pretty soon?"

The second day of their journey was drawing to a close, and still Dan had seen few signs of civilization. Now and then, he caught sight of a swirl of smoke and realized they were passing homesteads, but Luke was the only human he had encountered since leaving Melissa at the commissary weeks ago.

"I reckon as how we'll be there afore long. See that big pine tree yonder?"

Dan laughed. They were walking through a forest of hundreds of pine trees. "Yes, I see lots of them."

Luke didn't see the humor in his statement. "That big one right yonder that's had the top burnt out by lightnin'. It's sittin' just this side of that big bend in the creek."

"Yes, I see it. Is that where the store is?"

"Right around that curve, we'll come to it. Now, when we go inside, I want you to stick close to me, you hear?"

"Sure, Luke. I'm hoping I'll see somebody I know."

Luke eyed him curiously. "Your homestead close to here?"

"Um, not far," Dan said, hoping he was correct. With every step, the land looked more familiar. He wanted to run or at least walk at a faster pace, but Luke showed signs of fatigue as he struggled to keep up; and Dan didn't want to upset him. The man never let Dan forget that he walked behind him with two loaded rifles, and he had already proved to be an accurate shot.

When they finally rounded the bend, Luke pointed. "See? There she is: Joe-Tom's General Store."

Dan strained to see the building ahead, and his heart lurched. He had been here before! He remembered it well. Joe-Tom was his father's friend. And his mother bought supplies in that very store. The dark curtain in his mind began to rise, letting in a beautiful radiance of memories. It was all coming back to him now. For one brief moment, he forgot about Luke and his rifles as he broke into a run.

"Hey, stop that," Luke called, firing his rifle into the air. "You get back here, or the next bullet is yours."

Dan turned around. "Sorry, Luke. I just got a little excited. You see, I just remembered who I am and where I came from." His grin spread from ear to ear, all across his glowing face.

"You're talkin' like a crazy man. But I don't care what kind of story you conjure up, you ain't goin' nowhere till I get my *ree-ward*."

Dan could laugh now. Life was sweet. He led the way up the steps and into the weather-beaten storefront. He drank in the familiar sights surrounding him. Although he remembered each little detail of the store's layout, he didn't recognize the man at the counter. "Where is Joe-Tom?"

"He's gone home for supper. Can I help you, sir?"

Dan had forgotten about Luke until he heard the old man jumping up and down, shouting, "I knew it! I got him. That's him! I come for my *ree-ward*."

Dan turned to see Luke jerk a poster down from the wall and take it to the counter. Dan tried to get a closer look by peering over his shoulder, but Luke backed him up with the barrel of his rifle. "Stay back there, sonny. Now, just look at this and try to tell me that ain't you." He held the poster aloft, and the clerk came from behind the counter to see what all the commotion was about.

Dan saw a sketch that looked just as he had looked when he left home last January, a little heavier than now and clean shaven. "Looks like me all right. What does it say?"

Luke handed the paper to the clerk. "Here, you read it." Dan suddenly realized that Luke must not know how to read.

The baffled clerk held the paper and looked from Dan to the sketched likeness in his hands. "It says: *$100 reward for information on the whereabouts of Don Dupree, beloved son of Carson and Genela Dupree. Last seen on the second day of January 1840.*"

Dan was beside himself with joy. "That's my mom and dad. I remember it all now. Come on, Luke. I know the way from here. Come home with me, and if there's a reward, I'll see that you get it."

Luke looked at the clerk. "You mean he ain't done nothin' wrong? He ain't wanted by the law?"

The clerk shook his head. "No, this is the man everybody's been out looking for." He strode toward Dan and stretched out his hand. "I'm new around these parts, but I've heard plenty about you, Don. Welcome back!"

Luke lowered his rifle, disappointment clouding his face. "Don? He told me his name was Dan."

Dan didn't want to take time to explain. He just wanted to go home.

As they stood talking, another couple wandered into the store. The man in overalls and the lady wearing a calico dress with a matching sunbonnet walked right past them without a word, but suddenly the woman whipped around and shrieked, "Don Dupree! You're back!" She moved in for a closer look. Pointing her forefinger in his face, she said, "You ought to be ashamed of yourself! You've had your poor mother worried sick. Where have you been hiding out all this time?"

"Yes, ma'am. I'm glad to be going home again." Ignoring

her question, Dan edged toward the door. "Come on, Luke. We'd better get going."

Luke wiped his brow with a bandanna. He looked totally exhausted. "Are you sure that sign says there's a *ree-ward*? How much farther is it to this place of yours?"

"Not far. Maybe a mile. Here, now that you know I'm not an outlaw, let me carry my own rifle. I'll carry yours, too, if you'd like."

Luke shifted his burdens onto his young companion's shoulders, and the two of them left the store walking side by side.

☙

All week long, things in the Malcolm household were a veritable beehive. On Tuesday, Josie Ann rode over on her pony to show Melissa the dress her mother had made for the wedding. Josie Ann was to be Melissa's only attendant.

"I can't stay long. Mother wants me to hurry home and help her, but I couldn't wait to show you my gown." In Melissa's bedroom, Josie Ann slipped the dress over her head and twirled around. "Do you like it?"

"I love it! That soft blue dimity really brings out the highlights in your auburn hair. Your mother is such a talented seamstress."

"Help me get out of it before I get it mussed." With Melissa's help, she squirmed out of the gown and refolded it into a neat package. "I still can't get over your wedding coming before mine," Josie Ann exclaimed. "Why, the last time you were at my house, I told you all about my wedding plans, and you didn't even say you had a beau." She looked slightly miffed. "I thought we were best friends and shared everything."

Melissa helped her with the back buttons of her gingham frock and gave her a hug. "Of course we're best friends. It's just. . .well, it's all happened rather suddenly."

Josie Ann gasped. "Oh, Melissa! You're not. . ."

Melissa felt a rush of blood to her face. "Of course not. How could you even suggest such a thing?"

Now it was Josie Ann's turn to blush. "I'm sorry, Melissa. Of course I know you're not that kind of girl. It's just that it all came up so fast and all. You're still going to be a bridesmaid at my wedding in June, aren't you?"

"I'm planning on it."

"I'm so excited. I wish mine was this month like yours. I don't think I can wait until June. The circuit rider is certainly going to be busy when he gets here this time. Daddy said he has several weddings and new baby christenings to do before he gets around to me. You're lucky yours is first!"

"Mm."

"Well, I can see you're busy," Josie Ann said. "I'd better be getting back home myself. Mama wants me to help her get all our silver polished before our relatives start arriving for the wedding next month."

"It was nice of you to come, especially now when you're so busy getting ready for your own wedding. I'm happy for you, Josie Ann."

"As I am for you. I've known Mr. Blake since I was a little girl, but I never thought—I mean, well, he's so much older and all." Embarrassed by her blunder, she made matters worse by trying to make them better. "I mean, not that much older, really, and he's very nice. Of course age doesn't have anything to do with it when you fall in love, and, and. . ."

"It's all right, Josie Ann. You're right. He *is* a lot older than you and I."

Josie Ann, her cheeks flaming, almost tripped in her hurry to get out the front door. "I'll see you again on Thursday when I come for the rehearsal. I'm glad you invited me to stay overnight so I can get dressed for the wedding in your room." She unhitched her pony from the post and led him through the front gate. "Bye."

Melissa returned to the house to see if her mother needed help. It was good to see Mama so happy and energetic. She found her in the kitchen, singing as she worked.

Mama had covered the floor beneath the ironing board with a sheet to protect the frothy white gown from soil as she carefully pressed out every wrinkle. Standing in her stocking feet, she alternated between two irons, keeping one on the wood stove to heat while she worked with the other until it cooled. The kitchen was hot, but the fire in the stove was necessary for heating the irons. Every two or three minutes, she used a clean rag to mop her forehead, lest a drop of perspiration fall and spot the delicate fabric.

"I do declare, Melissa, I wish you could show a little more enthusiasm. I've worked my fingers to the bone on this dress, and I've yet to hear you say you like it."

"I'm sorry, Mama. Of course I like it. It's the most beautiful dress I've ever had." She kissed her mother's flushed cheek. "Here, let me finish that."

"No indeed," Mama protested. "You might scorch it. And mind you, don't get any dirt on that sheet you're walking on. You ought to take off your shoes before you come in here."

Melissa backed away. "I'm going out to the garden to pick some peas for supper, but I'll go out the front door and walk around the house so I don't have to walk through the kitchen on my way."

Mama gave an exasperated sigh. "Melissa, your wedding is only three days away. You ought to be soaking your hands in lemon juice to make them nice and white instead of dirtying them in the garden. And what about your hair? I've been collecting rainwater in the barrel for you. After you wash it, I'll curl it up in rags for you. Honey, if you'll just quit scowling and put a smile on your face, you'll be the prettiest bride in the whole Florida Territory."

Before Mama could give her any more advice, Melissa

grabbed a basket from the shelf, backed out of the kitchen, and headed for the garden.

She loved working in the garden. As she pulled the tender green pods from their vines, she remembered again how Dan had worked to till this soil for her. She felt closer to Dan in the garden than anywhere else. Some days she could almost feel his presence beside her.

She was glad he'd never know she was marrying Harrison Blake. She felt like a traitor, yet what choice did she have? Papa was right. She had been selfish to think only of her own happiness. She would go through with this marriage as her parents wished, but she didn't think she could smile about it. Not when her heart was breaking in two.

The rehearsal was scheduled for Thursday night. Papa had fashioned a gazebo in the backyard, and Harrison had sent two of his men to help construct benches for the guests to sit on. Every time Melissa passed the new construction, a shiver went up her spine.

In one corner of the yard, Papa had dug a big barbecue pit, where he planned to roast the pig Harrison had donated for the rehearsal supper.

The rehearsal supper wouldn't be nearly as elegant as the dinner party Harrison planned to host at his estate after the wedding. Melissa couldn't get used to the idea of referring to an evening meal as dinner. To her it was supper, and dinner was always served at noon. She had a lot to learn when she became Mrs. Harrison Blake.

When her basket was full, she sat on the back steps shelling peas into a blue-speckled enamel pan. If a few salty tears fell into the pan, no one would ever know the difference. And if the peas stained her fingertips, no one would care except her mother.

twenty-one

Dan wasn't prepared for the welcome he received when he walked unannounced through the front door of his family's rambling ranch house. Amid screams and squeals, laughter and tears, he was hugged by everyone once, and then they all started over again: his mother, his father, his sister, and his brother—even the bright-eyed Spanish cook! As though he had never been away, he recalled each face and each name— even his own! He was no longer Dan. He was Don Dupree, and he was *home*!

In all the excitement, he had almost forgotten his companion until he felt a gentle tug on his sleeve. "Ask 'em about the *ree-ward*," Luke reminded him. "And you reckon I could sleep in your barn tonight?"

Don pulled his little sister's arms from around his neck and turned to his friend. "I'm sorry, Luke. Of course we'll take care of you tonight, and tomorrow we'll have someone take you home on the back of a horse. How's that?"

"And the *ree-ward*, too?"

"Of course. I'll see to it myself."

When the excitement began to die down, Carson Dupree pulled his son down beside him on the davenport in the parlor and begged to hear every detail of Don's strange disappearance. "We were frantic after my men found Scotty's body up near Daniel Creek. We knew y'all had run into a band of outlaws, and we feared your body had been devoured by the wild animals that roam in the woods in that part of the territory. We had everybody out looking for you—even offered a reward."

"Oh, that reminds me, Dad. My friend Luke wants to

159

claim that reward." Don chuckled. "I reckon he deserves it if anyone does."

"We'll take care of Luke," Don's father assured him. "He's out back spinning tales with the cowhands right now. I think he's met his match. But we have more important things to talk about. We all want to hear what happened to you."

The dark cloud that had hovered over his mind for the past few months disappeared like a fog when the sun comes out. Suddenly Don could see the terrible scene as though it were being played out right in front of his eyes. His heart pounded against the walls of his chest. "It's a long, ugly story."

Genela Dupree leaned forward in her rocking chair. "Son, now that you're home, we've got all the time in the world."

"Scotty and I were riding through the woods on our way to Tallahassee to deliver the gold to the bank, when we were ambushed by a gang of outlaws. They must have known what we were carrying, because they demanded the gold we had in our saddlebags.

"We exchanged some shots, and I'm pretty sure I got one of their men, but then I heard one more blast before I started falling off my horse, and that's all I remember, until. . ."

"Yes? Go on," his father urged. "Have they held you captive all this time?"

Where should he begin to tell them of the last few months of his life? How could he explain his deep feelings for Melissa, or should he even try? "The Lord took care of me," he said. "It was a true miracle. He even sent one of His angels to look after me."

His eyes grew misty, remembering Melissa as he walked away and left her with tears streaming down her cheeks. He couldn't tell them about Melissa yet. He'd save that for later. "There's something important that I remember about that day. Something I haven't known until now. I know the leader of that outlaw gang, and I know just where to find him. And when I do. . ."

"Hold on there, Don." His father placed a hand on his knee. " 'Vengeance is mine, saith the Lord.' If you know where to find the scoundrels, we'll see they get what's coming to them, but we'll do things the right way. The United States marshal is already aware of your disappearance. I'll send a man to get in touch with him right away to let him know we've found you and to get an arrest warrant for the murdering thieves who did this thing."

Don jumped to his feet. "You're right, Dad, but there's something you don't understand. There's no time to waste. A girl's life may be at stake. A very special girl—the one who saved my life."

ﻉ

Melissa took a big iron pot of boiled potatoes off the stove and carried them to the back steps to drain the water from them. An aroma of roasting pork filled the air. She waved to her father, who was turning the spit over hot coals in the recently constructed barbecue pit, and he used his free hand to wave back.

Returning to the kitchen, she sat at the table to dice the potatoes for her salad, adding the eggs she had boiled and chopped earlier that morning.

"Don't forget the cucumber pickles," Mama reminded her. "I don't like potato salad without pickles in it. And I made fresh mayonnaise yesterday so we'd have plenty for your salad and my coleslaw."

Melissa worked with a heavy heart, while Mama chattered aimlessly. "I hope I baked enough biscuits. Melissa, do you think we have enough bread? I made corn bread, too."

"I'm sure there'll be plenty, Mama."

"Well, Harrison is bringing in some extra people. I didn't think I could ask him not to since he's provided the meat. Did you put those extra jugs of water in the springhouse? It's going to be hot, and we don't want to run out of cold water."

"Yes, ma'am. I squeezed the rest of those oranges, too, so we'll have plenty to drink. Quit worrying so, Mama. Everything will work out fine."

"Well, it isn't as if I had a daughter getting married every day. I mean, this is a very special day. Aren't you excited?"

Excited was not the word Melissa would have chosen to describe her emotions, but if it made Mama happy, what did it matter? "Oh, yes. Excited. As a matter of fact, I dreamed about the wedding last night." She scooped out a cup of mayonnaise and stirred it into her potatoes.

"You did? Oh, tell me about it."

"I had on the pretty new organdy gown you made for me, and I was walking across the yard toward the gazebo." She kept part of her dream to herself—the part where she looked up into the face of her handsome groom. But it was Dan's face, not Harrison's, that looked down and smiled at her. "I—I don't remember the rest."

"Well, I'm glad you're beginning to think about it anyway. For a while there, I was afraid you were unhappy about these arrangements. Melissa, you do know that your father and I both want your happiness, don't you? Everything we've done is for your ultimate good."

"Thank you, Mama." Melissa spread a tea towel over the top of her salad. "This is ready to set in the springhouse. Do you have anything else you want me to take?"

"Here. Take a few of these biscuits out to your papa." She opened the warming oven and took out three biscuits. "Spread some butter and jelly on them first. Tell him I won't have time to fix dinner today. With all the preparations for the rehearsal supper, I'm just too busy."

Melissa was glad for a chance to go outdoors. The heat in the kitchen was stifling, and Mama's constant chatter about the wedding and rehearsal only made her more nervous. She had only one more day to be simply Melissa Malcolm, a plain and unsophisticated country girl, and she wanted to enjoy every minute of it.

≈

By midafternoon, everything stood in readiness for the five o'clock rehearsal. Melissa filled her washbowl from the pitcher on her table to bathe before she put on a fresh skirt and blouse. Mama had told her that when she lived in Harrison's house, she would have a real bathtub, big enough to sit in and soak. She could hardly imagine such luxury. That was just one of the many advantages her mother continued to point out to her, but Melissa would gladly relinquish it all if she could have this wedding called off.

Once the preacher pronounced them man and wife, there would be no turning back, for the Bible clearly stated that when God joined them together, they should remain united until death.

A gentle knock on her door interrupted her thoughts, followed by Josie Ann's voice. "Can I come in?"

Her best friend looked radiant in a lime green dimity gown with a matching parasol. She carried a valise with her extra clothes. "May I hang my dress in your wardrobe?"

"Of course." Melissa took her valise and slid it beneath her bed. "Just put it there in my closet. It's truly beautiful."

Josie Ann shook the wrinkles from her gossamer blue gown and draped it over the rod in Melissa's oak armoire. "Who's going to stand in for you at the rehearsal this afternoon?"

"What do you mean?"

Josie Ann explained. "It's bad luck for the bride to rehearse. You have to appoint someone to act in your place, and you just sit back and watch." She giggled, letting Melissa know she was not truly superstitious but merely enjoyed observing an age-old custom.

Melissa privately wished someone could stand in for her at the actual ceremony. Instead of watching, she would like to fade off into the sunset. But of course, she couldn't tell Josie Ann that. "I've never heard that one. Well, it can't be you because you have to rehearse as the bridesmaid."

"That's true. You'll have to pick someone else. Hurry up and finish dressing. Let's go outside and see if the others are here yet."

Groups of people clustered in the backyard, most of whom Melissa didn't even know. She supposed them to be people Harrison had brought.

"There you are, my dear." Melissa cringed when Harrison stepped forward and reached for her hands, while onlookers smiled at the supposedly happy couple. "I've been looking for you. I'm hoping we can get this thing started before long. I find it very hot standing out here in the sun. Perhaps we should move over there under the shade of the oak trees."

Melissa pulled her hands free. "It doesn't matter to me, Harrison. I'll find Papa and ask him. He's the one who is organizing this thing."

"What's that? I think I heard my name." Papa walked over to them and put an arm around Melissa's shoulder. "Isn't she lovely? Harrison, you're a lucky man."

"I am that," Harrison agreed, ogling his bride-to-be from head to toe. His lecherous stare caused goose bumps to rise on her arms. "Say, Cleve, do you think we can go ahead and get started? How about moving over there in the shade?"

Harrison's word was law as far as Papa was concerned. "Of course. I wonder why I didn't think of that myself. Has the preacher arrived yet?"

"He's riding up now," someone shouted.

The scene was one of mass confusion until the Reverend Owen stepped up and took charge. He began to group people in their places, while onlookers sat on the benches Papa had made.

Papa and Harrison stood side by side in front of the preacher.

It was decided that Harrison's sister, Daisy, would play the part of the bride. The thirtyish spinster seemed delighted.

Melissa sank down on a bench among the guests, thankful she didn't have to participate because her knees were already shaking like a piece of isinglass in a hurricane. What would they be like by tomorrow?

The procession began as Josie Ann walked solemnly down the path to the makeshift altar. Next came one of Harrison's nieces, a precocious little redhead, vigorously tossing rose petals from a wicker basket to embellish the bride's earthen walkway.

The make-believe bride had just taken two steps, crushing the first of the delicate rose petals, when a posse of men rode into the yard. All eyes turned in their direction.

The man in the lead dismounted, and Papa strode forth to meet him. "Sir, just who do you think you are? We are in the middle of a wedding rehearsal, and I will not tolerate this interruption."

"Begging your pardon, sir." The gentleman opened his coat, displaying a large star on his chest. "I am a United States marshal."

"What is the meaning of this?" Papa demanded. "I don't care if you're the president; you have no right to be here without my permission."

"I'm afraid you are mistaken," the marshal responded. "I have every right. I am looking for a man by the name of Harrison Blake."

Harrison stepped forward, his face the color of yesterday's ashes. "I am he. Just what is your purpose in coming here at this inopportune time?"

Papa's mouth dropped open as he saw the marshal snap a pair of handcuffs on the man he had begun to think of as his son-in-law. The once-noisy crowd had grown as quiet as a cemetery.

"Harrison Blake, I have a warrant for your arrest."

"I'll have my lawyers see about this," Harrison protested. "I've done nothing wrong. What are these charges you've trumped up?"

"Robbery and murder."

Murder? The whispered word echoed through the crowd.

"You can prove nothing," Harrison insisted.

The marshal motioned to one of his men, who brought forth two leather saddlebags monogrammed with the letter D. "Do you recognize these?"

Harrison began to splutter. "No. I mean, yes, maybe. They look like some I found one day down around Daniel Creek. I've been trying to find out who they belong to."

"And what about the gold that was inside them?" the marshal persisted. "Were you also trying to find the owner of that?"

"The bags were empty when I found them," Harrison declared. "Just where did you get them, anyway? Have you burglarized my home?"

The marshal pulled a paper from his pocket. "We have a search warrant, Mr. Blake. We found a lot of interesting things at your place, like some of the cattle that've been rustled from your neighbors' pastures."

Harrison was sweating profusely. "Look, maybe some of my cow hunters might have stolen cattle without my knowledge. I'll look into it, and if that's the case, I'll see that the animals are returned to their rightful owners. Now, will you please take these things off my wrists so we can get on with our rehearsal?"

"I'm afraid I can't do that, Mr. Blake. The most serious charge here is murder. We've already taken two of your men into custody, and they've confessed to everything."

"They're liars. I had no part in any of this."

"And in addition to their confession, we also have an

eyewitness." He motioned to his men on horseback, who opened a pathway for the tail rider to come forward. "This is Mr. Don Dupree, and he says you shot and killed his partner."

A scream pierced the air, emanating from the center bench of onlookers. "Don Dupree? It's Dan!" Melissa staggered forward three steps before she slumped to the ground in a dead faint.

When she opened her eyes, she was in Don's arms and Mama was bathing her face with cool water. Papa stood over her, stirring up the air with a palmetto fan. "I must be dreaming again." But Melissa did not want the delightful delusion to end. She allowed her eyelids to fall shut and willed her dream to last forever.

twenty-two

"Isn't God good?" Melissa asked. "He's answered almost all my prayers in ways I never could have imagined." There was one He hadn't answered, but she hadn't given up hope on that one yet.

On a patchwork quilt spread beneath the oak trees, she sat beside Don, listening to him fill in all the missing pieces to the puzzle that had hovered over them for such a long time.

"I yearned to tell you how much I loved you before I left, but it wouldn't have been fair until I knew who I was and where I came from."

"On that last day, I saw a poster in the commissary with your picture, and I was pretty sure you were the one they were looking for," Melissa told him. "But I never could get anyone to believe me. By the way, did you know they solved the mystery of the commissary robbery?"

"Yes, it was that guy Clarence that used to drive the buggy for Harrison. Now I know how he got that shoulder wound."

"But how did the marshal tie him into the holdup at the commissary?"

Don shifted his weight to rest on one arm for a better view of Melissa. "While he was using the warrant to search the Blake ranch, he recognized the man whose picture he had seen on a wanted poster. He placed Clarence under arrest and called in Mr. Whittamore for a positive identification. Clarence was part of the gang that ambushed me, too, but he won't be causing any more trouble for a while. He's in custody now, along with several others from that outfit."

"That day when we parted at the commissary in Milltown

was the darkest day of my entire life," Melissa confessed. "It was terribly brash of me to ask to go with you, but I was desperate and didn't know what else to do."

"It was a hard moment for me, too. But that's all behind us now. Let's don't think about it anymore."

Melissa tried to erase from her mind the picture of him standing beside her wagon, ready to walk away from her forever. "How did you ever find your way home?"

Don told her the whole story of his long trek through the woods, his encounter with Luke, and even his scary confrontation with a black bear. "I've narrowly escaped death three times this year already. The Lord must surely have a plan for me."

"Of course He does. That's one of the first things you taught me when I gave you Granny's Bible to read. I guess your first narrow escape was when Harrison and his gang took your gold and left you for dead."

"Yes, and if you hadn't found me when you did, their plan would have worked. The second time I looked death in the face was when his henchmen came looking for me and almost burned down your barn. By the time I met up with that bear, I should have begun to get used to danger."

"Well, you're not out of danger yet," Melissa warned playfully. "You still haven't asked my father if we can get married."

Don guffawed. "Your dad and I have already become good friends. Cleve is thankful he found out about Harrison before it was too late. He feels guilty about his efforts to push you into marriage. Would you really have gone through with it, Melissa?" His eyes searched hers with such intensity that it pained her to answer truthfully.

"I'm afraid I would have," she admitted. "I didn't think I'd ever see you again, and nothing else seemed to matter."

He lifted her right hand to his lips and brushed her

knuckles with a gentle kiss. "Well, I'm here now, and I'm never going to leave you again. I can't wait to take you home to meet the rest of my family."

"Suppose they don't like me?" Worry wrinkles creased her forehead. "I'm just an ordinary country girl, Dan. . .er, Don."

Don used his fingertips to smooth the lines from her brow. "They love you already, my darling. I've told them all about you. And you're far from ordinary, Melissa. Now, about this wedding, it looks like you have everything all set up. You even have your wedding gown. Can't we just go ahead and have it right away?"

Melissa shook her head. "I'll never wear that gown," she declared. "It holds too many ugly memories. I'll pack it away in Mama's trunk, and maybe someday I'll tell my daughter how I almost threw my life away."

"*Our* daughter," Don amended. "I hope we have several."

"And about the wedding ceremony, please, I don't want to have it here. I don't want anything to remind me of the terrible mistake I almost made. We can be married anywhere, but not in that gazebo."

"If you don't want to be married here at your own home, how about my place? My parents would be delighted to have our wedding there on the ranch. We're situated on a big lake close to the Suwannee River. It's real pretty. But it's up to you. I'll go anywhere you want, as long as you promise you'll be mine forever."

He stood and pulled her to her feet. "Let's shake the leaves off this quilt and go find your parents. They might like to be included in these plans."

Hand in hand, the happy couple strolled across the yard, their shoes crushing faded rose petals that lay in their path.

epilogue

"Some people call this 'the singing river,'" Don told Melissa as they stood on the grassy bank, watching blue currents of the Suwannee roll by.

"I can understand why," she said, looking up into her fiancé's beautiful blue eyes. "Just listen."

Massive oaks stretched moss-laden limbs over the wide expanse of water. Overhead, the sound of songbirds was accompanied by the rippling trill of the beautiful singing river.

He led her up the bank and across a wide expanse of green lawn, where their new frame house rose against a backdrop of the setting sun. "Tomorrow I'll carry you over that threshold for the first day of the rest of our life together."

Was it really true, or was she dreaming again? "Mama made me a new wedding gown, and Papa even bought a suit for the occasion. He's made some wonderful changes in his life."

"Yes, now that he's accepted a position here on the ranch, it's made life a lot easier for your mother."

"That, too," Melissa admitted, "but I was referring to an even bigger change. An answer to one of my prayers."

He gave her hand a squeeze. "Yes, he told me how you and your mama finally opened his eyes to the Word of God. Now that he has accepted Christ as his Savior, he's changed into a new person, just like the Bible promises."

"He's happier than I've ever seen him," Melissa agreed. "And Mama has blossomed, too, now that she has him at home. The tenant house your father moved them into is just the right size for them and easy for Mama to take care of. Mama says it already feels like home."

"I hope she'll always feel that way, Melissa. Being lost and not knowing your way home is a terrible experience. I can certainly attest to that."

Don stooped to pick a small bouquet of wild daisies and placed it in her hands. Melissa smiled, remembering Harrison's many gifts of huge, fragrant roses and knew that these simple flowers were more beautiful by far. She lifted them to her face and buried her chin in them. "I was lost, too," she confided.

"You? I didn't know you were ever lost. When was that?" Don wrapped a protective arm around her shoulders as they walked toward the house.

"I was just like that poor little lost sheep in the Bible until you helped me find my way home."

He gave her shoulder an affectionate squeeze. "Now that we've both found the way, we'll keep Christ at the center of our lives, and we'll never be lost again."

A Letter To Our Readers

Dear Reader:

In order that we might better contribute to your reading enjoyment, we would appreciate your taking a few minutes to respond to the following questions. We welcome your comments and read each form and letter we receive. When completed, please return to the following:

Fiction Editor
Heartsong Presents
PO Box 719
Uhrichsville, Ohio 44683

1. Did you enjoy reading *The Way Home* by Muncy G. Chapman?
   ❑ Very much! I would like to see more books by this author!
   ❑ Moderately. I would have enjoyed it more if

   _____

   _____

   _____

2. Are you a member of **Heartsong Presents**?   ❑ Yes   ❑ No
   If no, where did you purchase this book? _____

   _____

3. How would you rate, on a scale from 1 (poor) to 5 (superior), the cover design? _____

4. On a scale from 1 (poor) to 10 (superior), please rate the following elements.

   ____ Heroine   ____ Plot
   ____ Hero   ____ Inspirational theme
   ____ Setting   ____ Secondary characters

5. These characters were special because? _____

_____

_____

6. How has this book inspired your life? _____

_____

_____

7. What settings would you like to see covered in future
   Heartsong Presents books? _____

_____

_____

8. What are some inspirational themes you would like to see
   treated in future books? _____

_____

_____

9. Would you be interested in reading other **Heartsong
   Presents** titles? ❏ Yes ❏ No

10. Please check your age range:
   ❏ Under 18   ❏ 18-24
   ❏ 25-34   ❏ 35-45
   ❏ 46-55   ❏ Over 55

Name _____

Occupation _____

Address _____

City, State, Zip _____

HEARTSONG
PRESENTS

If you love Christian
romance...

You'll love Heartsong Presents'
inspiring and faith-filled romances by
today's very best Christian authors...DiAnn
Mills, Wanda E. Brunstetter, and Yvonne Lehman, to
mention a few!

$10.⁹⁹

When you join Heartsong Presents, you'll enjoy 4 brand-
new mass market, 176-page books—two contemporary and
two historical—that will build you up in your faith when you
discover God's role in every relationship you read about!

Mass Market 176 Pages

Imagine...four new romances every four
weeks—with men and women like you who
long to meet the one God has chosen as the
love of their lives...all for the low price of
$10.99 postpaid.

To join, simply visit www.heartsong
presents.com or complete the coupon
below and mail it to the address provided.

- -

YES! Sign me up for Heartsong!

NEW MEMBERSHIPS WILL BE SHIPPED IMMEDIATELY!
Send no money now. We'll bill you only $10.99
postpaid with your first shipment of four books. Or for
faster action, call 1-740-922-7280.

NAME _____

ADDRESS _____

CITY _____ STATE _____ ZIP _____

MAIL TO: HEARTSONG PRESENTS, P.O. Box 721, Uhrichsville, Ohio 44683
or sign up at WWW.HEARTSONGPRESENTS.COM